STEALING Candy

STEWART LEWIS

sourcebooks
fire

Published by Sourcebooks Fire, an imprint of Sourcebooks, Inc.
P.O. Box 4410, Naperville, Illinois 60567-4410
(630) 961-3900
Fax: (630) 961-2168
www.sourcebooks.com

Library of Congress Cataloging-in-Publication data is on file with the publisher.

Printed and bound in the United States of America.
VP 10 9 8 7 6 5 4 3 2 1

For Rowan

Chapter 1

A giant, white snake of fog twists through the rolling hills of the campus, making it look slightly medieval. Even though I hate this place, Norwalk River School is like a glossy brochure come alive. The weathered brick buildings crawl with ivy; old oak trees perfectly surround a manicured quad; and the students, including my roommates (the Borings), are mostly overachievers trying to live up to the expectations of their parents. When they talk about Dad who chills with Obama or Mom who teaches at Yale or other Mom who's on the cover of *Anthropology Today*, I usually veer the conversation away from mine. Somehow a dead mother and a one-hit wonder father who wears guy-liner don't measure up.

I am walking with Fin the janitor, much to the chagrin of the ninth-grade girls and senior prefect boys passing us. Yes, Fin is my friend. Who cares? It's not like we're sleeping together. They wish.

"So, drama, right?" Fin says, knowing my schedule.

"Unfortunately. I am clearly meant to be behind the scenes."

"Not with a face like yours," Fin says in a totally un-creepy way.

"Yeah, that's me, Cover Girl."

"Well, remember what I told you? You should be more involved."

"Fin, I never asked to come here. I feel like I'm in a holding tank. I mean, I do well in my classes, but I only really feel like myself when I'm shooting or editing foot-age—or hanging out with you."

Fin starts to blush a little, and for a second he looks like a boy.

"I don't feel the pressure everyone here feels to succeed, to be like their parents, because I don't have parents. Well, I have a father, if you could call him that, but he's not really in my life. And I'm definitely not Ivy League material."

"Of course you are, if you want that."

"I just want something to happen, something else. I'm sick of going through the motions."

Fin laughs, as if my problems are a joke.

"Guess what? I think you're gonna be fine."

"Whatever."

We do a fist bump explosion, and I enter the Black Box, where my drama class is. The theater is supposed to be all indie and artsy, like something you would see in Greenwich Village, and it almost feels like that—until I see Mrs. Balshak, our drama teacher, who all the boys call Mrs. Ball Sack. She looks like Bette Midler but with a longer nose and no makeup. She's wearing a wrap dress and Birkenstocks, and she has this look of eagerness on her face that is off-putting.

I sit in my usual place in the back next to Max the Goth. I overhear some kids talking about the break-in that took place at the infirmary—apparently kids looking for drugs. Also, someone spray-painted *Dick Wakely Before He Dicks You* on the side of the gymnasium, referencing our somewhat tyrannical headmaster, Richard Wakely. They're discussing whether or not the two incidents were related. Frankly, I couldn't care less.

"OK!" Mrs. B claps her hands to silence everyone.

I mostly zone out while a girl with a black bob recites a

monologue about getting raped. It's clearly done for shock value and not authentic sounding. Mrs. B stops her halfway through, makes her hold a chair in the air above her head, and then tells her to continue the monologue. The girl starts to weep from exhaustion, but any tears are good tears as far as Mrs. B is concerned. She's an emotion whore.

The last part of the class is improv, and she calls Max the Goth and me first. I'm supposed to be his mother, catching him in a lie. We're not supposed to say what the lie is, just convey it obliquely. Mrs. B actually says that to us.

"Don't smirk at me," I say to Max, whose mouth is always smirking. "I know what you did."

"No you don't. You don't know me at all."

"Oh, yes, I probably do," I say, snapping out of character. "You come from money, but your parents ignore you. They've probably sent you to boarding school since you were prepubescent. The black clothes and the spiked bracelet are just armor. Inside is a scared little boy. No amount of lipstick, Marilyn Manson, or anime porn will ever change that. And if you're not gay yet, you probably will be."

Max looks at me, his jaw slack. I can see Fin in the doorway, holding a mop, shaking his head, and smiling.

"What the…" Max says, dumbfounded.

Mrs. B picks the next round and asks me to stay after class.

Max calls me a bitch under his breath, but he's kind of impressed.

After the next two groups go, class ends and everyone files out. The rape monologue girl comes up to me and says, "That was totally real. How did you know that stuff?"

"It's pretty obvious, actually. How do you know about rape?"

"I don't."

"Also obvious."

"Well, you don't have to be mean about it," she says, flipping her bob and walking away.

Mrs. B gives me a condescending look and asks me to sit down.

"You know, my first concert was your father's," she says like it's some revelation.

"Sorry to hear that."

She sighs like she's just a vessel for my attitude to travel through.

"Candy, I think maybe you're more like Max than you think."

"Honestly, I'm not like any of these kids."

"You want to talk about it?"

"No. I just want to go away sometimes. You know, disappear."

"Be careful what you wish for," she says, tightening her wrap dress.

We look at each other in some kind of staring contest. Eventually I lose, because her face is too open, too genuine. She really wants to help me. The thing is, she can't bring my mother back, and she can't try to take her place. The world is just a stage to Mrs. B. Real life is what I'm trying to navigate.

I go back to my room and start working on my latest film. It's a series of shots of Fin and his dog, set to music. The beginning is a long shot through the glass door, so as the dog jumps up for his treat, it looks like he's also jumping through the bushes outside Fin's kitchen. Film is all about reflection. In a good film, ten minutes shouldn't pass without viewers seeing some kind of reflection—through a mirror, the side of a building, the lenses of a character's sunglasses. It speaks in metaphor without hitting you over the head and adds a layer of visual depth to a scene. I'm not sure where this film is going; I just know it's pleasing to watch. It's more about how it makes you feel than the content itself. Like the plastic bag in *American Beauty*.

"That's cool," one of the Borings says over my shoulder. "That dog is adorable."

I was going for nuanced or majestic, but I probably

shouldn't expect anything more than *adorable* from one of the Borings.

"Thanks," I say feebly.

"So, who do you think did it? The senior day students?" she asks, referring to the break-in and the vandalism.

"Some kids desperate for attention, I guess."

She looks at me, and a daze washes over her face. Then she walks back to her bed where her homework is spread out.

When lights-out comes, I can hear the Borings whispering. I'm sure they are talking about something really intellectual like lip gloss or some boy's lame ponytail. I know I don't belong here, but I also don't want to be back in Oakland. I think about Max the Goth and why I felt the need to call him out. Does it mean I like him? *God no.* Was Mrs. B right in saying that I was projecting? Maybe.

When I finally fall asleep, I dream of an open road that bends and climbs, eventually disappearing into the horizon. There's a girl smiling, wind in her hair. I'm pretty sure it's me. The world outside NRS is beckoning, big and complex and beautiful. But when I wake up, I can still hear Mrs. B's voice in my head.

Be careful what you wish for.

Chapter 2

The fog is still clinging to the ground. I am walking toward the dorms from the dining hall, pretty much by myself as usual, when a hand grips me above my elbow and yanks hard. In a split second, I'm in the backseat of a car that smells like sweat and gasoline. The first thing I think is that it must be some kind of prank. The kids that broke into the infirmary? The car is not a black van like in a horror flick or a shiny SUV like in a contemporary thriller. It's a faded red Toyota. The shattered rearview mirror has cracks spreading through it like tiny tree branches.

Before I can even react, the guy in the pa~
turns and shoves a ski mask over my head. I see his ey
for a split second: black, with a piercing shine, pupils shaking. My world goes dark, and then he duct-tapes my wrists
behind my back.

The mask is backward, so there are no holes for my eyes,
but the fabric is thin enough that I can breathe. As the
car peels out through the slush by the curb, I hear some
random girl yell, "Oh my God!"

Then I am pushed down onto the floor of the backseat.

What the…

The air is thick with urgency—something is telling me
it's not a prank. The nasty smell in the car is making me
nauseous. I can feel the soup I had at lunch swishing around
my stomach, threatening to come up.

What the hell is going on?

It's the day before winter break in my junior year of
boarding school, and I'm being abducted. As the car gains
speed, I can picture the buildings of campus—the spire
of the chapel, the ancient dining hall, the huge colonial
houses that act as dorms—getting smaller and smaller, now
probably enveloped in the fog.

As we take a sharp right out of the school's main gates,
questions blink in my brain like fireflies: *Who are these*

people? Is it really me they want? Where are we going? Why were his pupils shaking?

I start thinking about my homemade films on my laptop in my room, the tea I was drinking, left on my desk…

"Where are you taking me?" I manage to say, shifting my body to get a little more comfortable, if that's even possible on the floor of a backseat. I wonder if anyone is even following us. I doubt it—the security at NRS is kind of a joke. They're not going to do anything except call the police, and probably too late.

Fin. Maybe he can help…

Fin and I share a love of movies, and we hang out a lot at his crappy house down the street from campus, which we are probably passing now. I relate to him more than to the Borings, who study constantly and iron their pajamas, or the girls in my dorm with names like Bree and Gwen who excel at sports and obsess over where they're going to college— "Brown? No way, Williams." Yes, he is probably the father figure I never had, but he's on my level too. He looks out for me. I'm hoping maybe he saw the car. He seems to be omnipresent, like some kind of white-trash god.

I can't stand dead air, and since no one's speaking in the car, I do.

"You realize I already saw both of you, right?"

One of them turns up the radio, which is playing a country song. (Something Lana Del Rey would be way more appropriate—this twangy, three-chords-and-the-cheese song is taking the whole scene from Tarantino to Lifetime.)

The passenger strikes a lighter, and tobacco smoke immediately infuses the already-stale air.

I start to describe them, so they know that I'm not bluffing.

"Cancer Stick over here is riding shotgun. Six feet... African American the correct term? Someone told me we could just say black now. Anyway, tattoo of a blurry rose behind his ear—super original. I'm surprised it doesn't say 'Mom' on it or some crap."

That's when I feel it. A fist on the side of my head with enough force that my ears start ringing. "Ow!" I yell. I can't hold my head 'cause my hands are tied. I tell myself not to cry, but the tears have minds of their own.

I never cry. Not since my mother died a long time ago. I grew up with my grandmother Rena, who doesn't do emotions. But this is different. I was just punched in the head. Hard.

When the ringing finally subsides, the car is quiet, except for the whir of the wheels and my heart, which is smashing against my chest. I can hear Cancer Stick laugh, but it sounds more like a snicker. Flashes of kidnapping films flip through my mind in a kind of cinematic Rolodex. *Along Came a Spider, Don't Say a Word, Funny Games.* I start counting in how many of them the girl dies. But this is more real than a movie could ever be. There's a dent in my head, there are tears drying on my cheeks underneath the mask, and I may not make it out of here alive.

Is this about Wade?

My father, Wade Rex, is the lead singer of a band called the Black Angels. I call them the Butt Crack Angels. Even though they're all pushing fifty, they still party like the rock stars they were twenty years ago. My father wrote their one hit, "Spill It on Me," which is actually pretty good music-wise, but the lyrics are lame. Still, the song has basically subsidized my life, even though I haven't seen my father in years. I get tuition, random gifts, or a two-minute phone call once in a while, but the guy is basically a narcissistic tool. Also known to be impulsive and pea brained, which I'm guessing is the reason I'm bound in the back of this smelly Toyota. *Bound*, that's another kidnapping film. *Did she die?*

I try to take long breaths to slow down my rapid heart-beat, but it's not working.

"Is this about my father? 'Cause he doesn't care about me."

Cancer Stick reaches over and wraps his hands around my neck, pulling me up on the seat.

"Shut. The. Fuck. Up," he says, thrashing my head around with each word. He lets go, and I start to gasp for air. Now I'm shaking.

"Enough," the driver says, but he doesn't sound that concerned. The one thing I noticed about him was that he was sort of smiling. A half smile. I take more long, deep breaths. My throat is burning. *Cellular. Taken. Where's Liam fucking Neeson right now?*

Judging by how much we've picked up speed, we must be on Route 2.

Yes, my mother died and my dad dropped me off at my heartless grandmother's house, but nothing like this has ever happened to me. It's starting to sink in.

They are hurting me.

They are taking me away.

Chapter 3

For the next few miles, I just listen to the drone of the engine and try to breathe normally, but it's not easy. I think the guy damaged my throat. Tears start to thrum at my eyelids again, but I don't let them out. I have to try to be strong. I start to hum a little, but it sounds more like a whimper. I don't believe in God, but I start to pray. *Don't let me die with these losers. Please, whoever is out there, help me.*

I must have passed out for a while, because when I come to, we seem to be at a rest area. I can tell by the other car doors opening and closing, children laughing. Cancer Stick gets out, but Half Smile stays. I don't know if it's safe to talk again, but I have to when I'm nervous. Otherwise I'll explode.

"So...I saw you from a glimpse through the broken rearview. What junkyard did you hot-wire this ghetto-ass car from?"

I've never been this nervous before, and the words seem to leave my mouth on their own accord. He doesn't answer, but he also doesn't stop me, so I keep talking. "You've got black hair to your shoulders that you cut by yourself. Seventeen, maybe a little older. Definitely young for a kidnapper."

He makes what I hope is a conciliatory grunt.

"Where are we going? An abandoned warehouse? A drafty barn?"

He makes another noise, but I still can't tell if he's warming up to me or not.

"Is it money you want? I don't get all the royalties until I'm eighteen. That's almost two years from now. Oh, and I was serious: Wade couldn't care less about me. Once, when I was little and crying, he told one of his assistants to 'turn that thing off.' Touching, huh?"

Half Smile still doesn't say anything, but I feel like he's listening. This must be about Wade.

"That guy, Cancer Stick. He looks really cracked out."

"Shh," Half Smile says, but not very forcefully.

"Isn't this where I try to flirt with you or scream or something?"

This time I think I hear a chuckle.

I shift a little and realize my HD mini handheld is in my back pocket.

Even with my hands taped and my vision blocked, I manage to take it out and start filming my surroundings. Maybe it will be evidence. Half Smile doesn't say anything, so he's obviously not watching.

The door jerks open, and it startles me. I put the camera away quickly, praying he didn't see it. Cancer Stick is breathing weird through his nostrils. I know I shouldn't talk, but I have to. It's automatic, like someone slipped a quarter into my slot.

"If you're going south, I'd go west first to get into upstate New York."

Cancer Stick lunges over the seat and punches me in the stomach. My breath is taken away for an instant, and I see flickering stars in the corners of my vision. Then I throw up.

"I said, *Shut UP*. Or I'll put you in the trunk."

"Hey," Half Smile says. "We need her in one piece. Stop."

Now I can barely breathe, there's vomit inside my mask, and I can't stop my tears, which make my mask itch even more. It's hard to get me speechless, but now I am. My whole head feels numb.

What did Half Smile mean by in one piece? *Alive, right? They can't kill me. Please don't let them kill me...*

We start driving again, and I picture the yellow dashes coming and going, marking more and more distance from NRS. Thoughts ricochet back and forth in my addled brain.

Cancer Stick wasn't even gone long enough to go to the bathroom, or was he? Maybe he was making a phone call I couldn't listen in on. Something is going on with him. His vibe is so different than the driver's. And he's much older. Which one is my actual kidnapper? Is one of them just hired help? These things can go massively wrong. I could end up just another young body dumped on the side of the road.

Here comes my heart again, slamming like someone locked in a room and desperately trying to get out. Whatever I threw up is now dripping off my neck onto the floor of the car. I listen to the engine and try to un-freak myself out. They obviously need me alive. Although Cancer Stick seems really volatile. In addition to the bad tattoo and the shaking pupils, I saw a scar on his face the size of a large fingernail, between his left eye to his ear. I bet he's killed

17

someone, like, for sport. *Ransom. Panic Room.* Both kids, both made it. *Keep breathing.*

The radio gets turned on again, and it's some vacuous pop song. I can almost picture the video, a Barbie-like chick with caked-on makeup, touching her body and lip-syncing, pouting like a child. Even though the song sucks, it takes me out of my head and I am happy for the distraction. But it doesn't last long. My body is aching. My head still hurts, my throat is sore, and the vomit has mixed with my tears, both drying on my neck. Several miles later, they pull over again after Cancer Stick says he needs to go "number two."

"Number two?" I whisper to Half Smile after Cancer Stick once again leaves. "What is he, five?"

Half Smile chuckles this time.

"Looks like we got a comedian in here," he says under his breath like he's talking to himself.

"Listen, you think I can get a breath of air, just while Cancer Stick is having potty time? This mask is itchy, and I've got puke on me. Where's the mask from, anyway? Kmart? You could've splurged for Patagonia."

"I don't know…"

"Look. 'Keep your friends close but your enemies closer.'"

"What the…" I hear a slight gasp. "You know *The Godfather?*"

"All of them by heart."

"Hmm," he says, reconsidering me.

"I've already seen you," I say, even though I've mostly seen the other one.

"OK, just for a minute."

I feel his hands, which are soft, not callused, peel up the mask to just above my mouth. My breathing gets easier, and I resist the urge to talk more. I can feel a charge in the air, but I'm not sure what it is. *Is he studying me?*

"Look, don't provoke him," Half Smile says, wiping my mouth and neck with a rag.

I nod, and we sit there in screaming silence. I have no idea what is going to happen to me, but I know that the simple act of him moving my mask up and wiping me clean means something. When I hear Cancer Stick's footsteps getting closer to the car, my whole body stiffens, as if instinctually preparing for him to hit me again.

The driver reaches over and slides the mask back down.

Now I'm actually smiling underneath it.

The car merges back onto the highway. I hear a crack of thunder in the distance and some crows cawing.

My mother once told me that the road is a chance. I didn't know what she meant, but it sounded nice. She died when I was seven. She had long arms that swayed when she walked and the kind of face you wanted to trust. She was a Black Angel groupie who ended up sticking around after Wade got her pregnant. She raised me in tour buses, back-stage green rooms, and hotel suites. I loved how everything was always changing—it didn't bother me because I never had a stationary life to compare it to.

After she died, I was sent to live with my grandmother Rena in Oakland. When I arrived there, Rena met me at the door, handed me a rake, and told me to start on the leaves that were scattered across the lawn in front of her old Tudor house that smelled like mothballs and stale coffee grounds. "Nice to see you too," I had said. To this day, the woman has never hugged me. She's the queen of tough love. I call her Meana. The only time I saw her show emotion was when we watched *I Am Sam* and a single tear cut down her cheek. She intercepted it halfway with her pinkie finger like it had never happened.

Still, I can picture her face when someone from school calls her, which they're probably doing right now. She may even drop the vintage coffee cup that's always in her hand. Though she's lame at showing it, she's the only one who actually cares about me. After that day of leaf-raking, I started watching the trains behind her house. It was the only thing that settled the whirlwind of my thoughts. I wish I could watch trains right now—or watch anything.

If I try to open my eyes, all I can see is a close-up mesh of black fabric, a big blur.

The radio gets switched again, and this time it's some band from England, probably with a one-word name. I can tell from the singer's voice that he's got a wave of retro hair and is wearing skinny jeans. Predictable, but I listen, trying to escape again, if only for three minutes.

Four songs later, we pull over and Cancer Stick gets out.

What is he doing that he can't do in the car?

Still, I'm glad to be alone with Half Smile again.

"Do you think I could just ride in the back like a normal person?" There's desperation in my voice that doesn't even sound like me. "If anything happens, I'll pretend to be your little sister or something. I don't want to go back to boarding school anyway. Especially if wherever we're staying has HBO."

He barks out a laugh that I hope is genuine and not mocking me.

A few minutes later, he says, "Hang on," and gets out of the car to talk to Cancer Stick, who has returned. I can hear their conversation. Half Smile's telling him I should just be a regular passenger, that he doesn't think I'll do anything stupid.

"It looks wrong. Someone will notice," he says.

Cancer Stick makes an agitated noise that sends a shudder through me.

"Fine, but if anything happens, I'll make sure it won't matter that she saw us, understand?"

I feel a dark wave of nausea in my stomach as images from my life flicker inside the lids of my eyes. My mother's delicate hands, the roads of America, the backstage food, the roar of crowds, the never-ending plains on each side of the bus, Fin and his dog, the trains in Oakland, Rena's coffee-stained lips.

I think about what I would leave behind if I died. *A music video and a few films? Some legacy. No, there's a lot more I have to do. And the first thing is to not let Cancer Stick kill me.*

They both get back in the car, and Half Smile moves me up into the seat. He doesn't jerk me around like Cancer Stick, but he's not exactly gentle.

My mask gets ripped off, and I blink against the bright world.

Cancer Stick gives me a cold, surly stare. The scar near his eye seems to be pulsing, and his pupils are now tiny, sunken almost all the way into the black hole of his eyes.

I look over at Half Smile, who looks surprised. But honestly, I'm the one who's surprised. His black hair falls in curved lines, and his eyes are such a light green that they look lit from behind. We stare at each other as he attempts to rip the duct tape off my wrist. It's not coming off, so he bites it with his teeth. The tiny hairs on my arms bristle, and I take an involuntary sharp intake of breath.

"Don't fucking try anything," he says.

I'm not sure what my face is doing, but I try to be as serious as possible and nod.

The road is a chance.

Chapter 4

As we drive, I can't stop looking at Half Smile. He's kind of rugged for a teenager, but also strangely elegant. His forearms are sinewy, with a soft pattern of light-brown hair. His lips are full and resting in a position that could be boredom, anger, sadness, or all three. His fashion choices are wrong in the right way: checkered shirt that's too preppy for him and one of those H&M wraparound leather cuff bracelets that freshman wear.

Cancer Stick keeps looking at me through the side mirror, his mouth a frozen, rigid line, his eyes half-dead. I move to the middle of the backseat to get out of his mirror's view. Looking in the broken rearview, I feebly try to fix my hair, which has become matted by the mask and still has some puke in it.

I was right—we're heading south, entering the Mass Pike in Hartford, the random city of drug addicts and insurance salesman. As we go through the toll, I think about trying to signal the attendant. But what happens when I'm rescued? Back to NRS with the Borings? It is better now that I'm not bound on the floor. But what if Cancer Stick has another freak-out? I've seen it a million times in the movies. I glance at the reflection of the blurred trees in the window and then close my eyes. Is it weird to see this as an adventure, a vacation of sorts?

I've actually never been on a vacation. Rena's idea of one is going to the dilapidated movie theater in Oakland. Movies are the one thing we do together as a family, if you can call it that. *Bitter, War-Torn Grandmother Bonds with Rejected Daughter of Rock Star.* She likes chick flicks, believe it or not, but I don't know how much she really understands. In English, she speaks two-word sentences. In Russian, she's like a windup toy, blabbering a mile a minute, whether it's to the bald guy at the corner store or her cousin who lives in Ohio. She never gave Wade much love either, which is probably why he's not exactly running for Father of the Year. These things are cyclical.

My nerves are still shot but also fueled by the complete unknown. It's a crazy thought, but maybe I needed something like this to wake me up.

"This is going to sound crazy, but it *is* nice to be away from school."

Cancer Stick looks back and squints at me, like he can't believe I'm still talking.

"I'm sorry, it's my nerves. Talking helps."

"Yeah? Well, you can't talk if you're dead."

He says it seriously but also like it's nothing.

I move completely behind Half Smile and start counting the white dashes on the road. I'm thinking Cancer Stick was just talking out of his ass, but I'm not willing to find out. They've already taken off my mask, so I really should shut up.

The day I was dropped off in Oakland, I was actually glad Rena made me rake the leaves. I felt useful. It took me hours, and when I was done, I thought maybe she'd cook me a meal or at least offer me a soda, but all she did was inspect the lawn and motion for me to come inside. There were stale, tasteless crackers and a hideous orange ball of cheese with sad little nuts clinging to it. "Wow, super gourmet," I told her, and she just stared back at me, her lips pursed. To this day, Rena doesn't get sarcasm.

Cancer Stick lights another smoke, and I can feel his black eyes on me through the rearview. I should be freaking out. Crying or shaking like before—or screaming for help. I'm being kidnapped. The wild thing is, my heart is not only pounding with fear but also with a twisted freedom.

We pull off the highway and up to a Burger King drive-through window. The clerk is a slightly effeminate kid with red hair and pudgy hands. As we order, he gives me a peculiar glance, like he's not sure what I'm doing in this beat-up car with these two guys. Or maybe he just knows that, like him, I have spots and stripes. Yes, I go to a posh boarding school and he probably lives in lower-income housing, but we will always be the same. We are outsiders. We exist on the periphery.

He gives us our food, and we pull over to the corner of the parking lot.

It's clear that Cancer Stick wants to do something. He doesn't touch his burger. He's fidgeting, his face is twitching, and tiny drops of sweat form a razor-thin line above his upper lip. I hope he's not planning on robbing the Burger King or drowning me in a river. *Cabin by the Lake*—many drowned girls.

Half Smile and I both eat with fervor while Cancer Stick gets more and more agitated. I watch him dump a sugar packet onto his tongue, and all of sudden I'm not hungry anymore. I'm scared. This guy is not playing mean or crazy. He is exuding it. I can almost smell it. Still, it's completely addicting, the waiting for what will happen next. I wanted something different, and here it is.

"So," I say, "please tell me you're not going to feed me to alligators or cut off one of my fingers."

Cancer Stick turns and says, "*Shh*," really loudly, like he's about to slap me again.

"Sorry," I whisper.

Half Smile actually smiles fully, and it changes his whole face. He's still handsome, but it makes him seem more vulnerable and less cool.

Cancer Stick turns, giving Half Smile a cold glare.

"Outside. Now."

They get out and begin talking next to the car. I don't look at them, but I overhear Cancer Stick spit out Half Smile's name: Levon. It's exactly the type of name I pictured he had. There's no way he would've been a Brian—or a Tom, even. A name like Levon suits him.

After a minute, Cancer Stick slams his hand down on the top of the car, which makes me jump up in my seat. Some kids who had been playing run back inside their minivan. The argument turns into shouting, and then they're suddenly still for a moment. I look over, expecting Cancer Stick to punch out Levon, but Levon reaches in his pocket and counts out a wad of bills. He holds it out to Cancer Stick, who grabs the cash and storms away. I sit back slowly, praying he's gone for good.

Levon gets in, sighs, then looks out the window, distracted. At the end of the parking lot, I watch Cancer Stick hail a cab.

"Was that a good-bye?" I ask.

"No. He needed to go get something."

"Wow. I don't even want to know what that might be."

Cancer Stick looks back at us before he gets in the cab. His black eyes seem to be searing directly into me. I lower my head.

A few seconds later, Levon starts the car.

Then he turns and looks at me like he's really noticing me for the first time.

He's not smiling, but his eyes are alive.

Chapter 5

We drive past the industrial wasteland of south Hartford. Low concrete buildings, abandoned cars, bits of trash swept up by the swirling wind. I wonder if we are going to New York City. One time, I stayed in a suite above Central Park, and from the vantage point of a super-high floor, the trees looked like bunches of broccoli a giant would eat, the black ponds reflecting white, puffy clouds. It seemed so pastoral and at odds with the putrid smells on the street, the loud sirens and trucks, and people yelling at each other. For some reason, it seemed like everyone in New York was having an argument. But maybe they were just really loud.

I held my mother's hand supertight as we walked to the venue where my father was playing. During the performance, we were backstage as usual, except for the last song, when she would usually leave me with a guy they called Wigger. I'm not sure what his job was, except for hanging out with the band. He always gave me lollipops, so I was fine with it. But I would anxiously wait for the final roar of applause, because I knew my mother would come back, and she always did.

Until one day she didn't.

Levon and I don't say anything for a while, but I sneak glances at the muscles on his forearm, tense from gripping the wheel. I'm not as scared now, more out of body, like I'm watching myself from above. I can't seem to shake Cancer Stick's crazed stare out of my brain—or the sound when his fist hit my head, where I can still feel a slight ache.

As we head toward the smokestacks of New Haven, I decide to try to get some information out of Levon. *At least I know he won't punch me. Or would he?*

"So, tell me this: Is it money you want?"

He doesn't answer, but he looks at me like, *What do you think?* Obviously he wants money. I reach in my pocket and count the change.

"I've got eighty cents," I say.

He chuckles again and turns off the highway, pulling into a place called the Painted Crow motel. I'm glad to see the free HBO sign, even though the light behind the *B* has gone out, so it reads FREE H O.

Levon parks, clears his throat, and says, "OK, let's move."

We both get out, and I follow him into the lobby. There's a girl behind the counter with a serpent tattoo crawling up her neck. She's eating a microwave burrito, and her phone has a faded skull on it. She doesn't look at me, but she smiles at Levon when he says he wants a room with two beds. I'm guessing Levon isn't into the serpent-chick type. *But what type would he be into?*

I let him lead the way out of the lobby to the rooms that open onto the parking lot. Each room has a faded green plastic chair outside it. We pass a fat woman smoking and two kids with dirt on their faces, looking guilty. I film them secretly by tucking my handheld into my sleeve. The film will come out upside down, but it's easy to switch in post.

Room 109 has wood paneling on the walls. It smells like bleach, and there's a painting of a lion jumping out of a bush, except the perspective is off.

"That would be a cool name for a band," I say, sitting on the farthest bed from the door, the one my mother always chose. "Bad Hotel Art."

He doesn't smile, but his face softens. He pulls two brand-new toothbrushes out of his weird, shiny green backpack. For a moment, my heart plummets and I can feel a shift, like I'm teetering on a precipice. Emotional vertigo.

I barely know this guy.

He is giving me a toothbrush from a strange, green backpack.

And his partner, who is coming back, hurt me.

"What's the deal with your bag?"

"It was a gift."

I shift back to safety, away from the edge, at the sight of his face proudly defending the backpack. He hands me one of the toothbrushes.

"You came prepared."

"Except I don't have any toothpaste."

"Hmm, that's kind of how it works. We can get some tomorrow."

A hint of surprise comes over his face, like he can't believe I'm not resisting or being difficult.

There's a cot in the corner of the room, which I assume is for Cancer Stick. The thought makes me tremble.

After a few minutes, Levon finally starts to talk, and it's like a river breaking through a dam. The words flow out in a rush.

"We're going to Miami. It's better if you don't ask me

too many details and just go along for the ride. We can get you some clothes and some snacks or whatever for the road. Just do what we say, stick to the plan, and nothing bad will happen. Got it?"

"Got it. Just tell me one thing. It's about my father, right?"

He pulls back his bedspread and throws it into the corner, then looks at me. "Duh," he says flatly.

"Look, I don't doubt it. My dad's a royal A-hole."

Levon makes a little noise, and I study his face. His features come together like a car crash—long nose, wide-set eyes, lavender-tinted lips. Separately they're average, but as a whole, they're extraordinary.

He throws one of his pillows on the cot. I wonder if he's actually friends with Cancer Stick. I hope not. The closest thing I've had to friends are Fin the janitor and Billy Ray, the boy who stalked me through middle school. Because I was Wade's daughter, Billy Ray thought I was God by relation. I never had the heart to tell him that Wade was not the hero Billy Ray thought he was. Not even close. But we had a mutual appreciation for watching the trains in Oakland, and I shot a video for his lame band, Tap Water. The video was cool, but the song wasn't even listenable.

I keep my clothes on and sit on the bed, turning on the TV. Levon goes into the bathroom to wash his face but leaves the door open so he can keep an eye on me. The news comes on, and at the end of a segment, I see my face. It's my NRS junior picture. I'm smiling facetiously, wearing a white T-shirt with a black star on it. For some reason, I'm not even shocked to see my face on TV. It's more like a quiet thrill. I wonder if the Borings are watching this. I know Fin isn't, because he doesn't own a TV.

Obviously, it was bound to happen. The newscaster, an earnest Asian woman, says something about "rock star royalty abduction" but I'm concentrating on the zit that's on my forehead. I don't consider myself a vain person, but this picture is definitely not my best moment. I'm grateful Levon isn't watching. The anchor mentions a number to call if anyone has any information. I film the TV when the number comes up, just in case.

When Levon comes out, he's in his boxers. I start counting the ridges of his abs—there are eight of them. While he turns to watch the sports segment, I sneak a video of his naked upper half, washed in the TV light. His skin is creamy and smooth. I try not to stare at the deep grooves on each side that run from his lower stomach to his crotch area. He gets under the covers in his own bed and pulls two pictures out of his worn wallet.

"Girlfriend?" I ask, trying to sound casual.

"Yes," he says in an end-of-conversation tone. I don't pry, but I find myself wondering who's on that small square of paper he's holding up to the light. *A blond cheerleader type? A skinny girl with glasses in a room full of books? Am I actually jealous? I don't even know the guy. Besides, he hasn't looked at me with any hint of sexual innuendo. Surprise and maybe a hint of laughter, but nothing even suggesting romantic.*

The other picture is worn at the edges, and I can sort of see it as he holds it up. It looks like an elderly woman, probably his grandmother.

HBO is playing a rerun of *The Sopranos*, the episode where Tony sees the geese in his pool.

"This is probably one of the most famous television episodes ever. Even more so now that James Gandolfini died," I say.

Levon puts away his pictures and looks at me.

"The thing about Tony Soprano is he had so many layers," I continue. "Like, the guy kills people but then cries like a baby over some geese."

"Yeah," he says, turning out the light.

"What about you. Kidnapper who carries a picture of Grandma?"

It's too dark to tell, but I think Levon is blushing a little.

He turns toward me and starts to say something but then looks back to the TV. By the time the credits roll, he is asleep. I could easily leave right now, before Cancer Stick comes back. But I don't have any money, and this is not a great part of town. I go into the bathroom, turn on the water, and film myself with my handheld.

"My name is Candy Rex. I've been kidnapped, and I'm somewhere south of Hartford in a red Toyota."

When I open the door, Cancer Stick is sitting on the cot, rolling an unlit cigarette through his fingers. I let out a yelp, and Levon tosses a little but doesn't wake up. My handheld is sticking out of my front pocket. I turn sideways so Cancer Stick can't see it and walk toward the bed. I get under the covers with my clothes on, and he's still looking at me. I swear there's a smirk on his face. My heart starts up again, like a loop on an EDM track. He looks as if he's on some kind of hard drug. He watches me for what seems like an eternity—but is probably twenty minutes—and then heads outside.

Levon is awakened by the sound of the door closing, and he gets up and joins him. I can hear them arguing again, and then Levon comes back inside, alone.

"What's up with him?" I whisper.

"Forget it. Go to sleep."

I cover my head with a pillow and think, *What would my mother do?* Would she have run by now, or would she go along for the ride? I miss her in my body, my bones. I never thought you could physically ache for someone. Certain memories pop into my head, like when she made this elaborate rainbow out of color-coordinated Froot Loops. She was always making things—out of anything, really. Like films are for me, creating art was what plugged her into the world.

Mostly, the things she made were for me: a giant pinwheel out of diner straws, a marshmallow Christmas tree, a flip book of drawings that showed birds leaving a nest, one by one. My first seven years of life were completely shaped by her presence. There were always flowers around her. In her hair; on her impossibly thin, print dresses; painted on the backs of her hands. Every time I see a lily or even a dandelion, I feel a sharp pang.

Levon is fast asleep again. He makes a soft puffing sound with every other breath. His left foot wiggles a little, like a dog dreaming. His elegant lips rest in his signature half smile.

I'm in a strange room, with a stranger.

I could call the help line or Rena or someone to come get me. But I don't. I just stare at the ceiling, frozen.

I keep waiting for Cancer Stick to come back, but he doesn't.

I have no idea how I'm going to sleep, even though I'm exhausted. I close my eyes, trying to block out the image of the empty cot in the corner.

Please don't let him come back. Please...

Chapter 6

When I wake up in the morning, Levon is already showered and dressed, his hair combed. He seems like he's been sitting there, waiting for me to wake up. He has placed a banana and a Styrofoam cup of orange juice at my bedside.

"I'll be outside in the car when you're ready," he says, then gets up to leave and shuts the door quietly, as if I'm still sleeping.

The cot is still made, but I half expect Cancer Stick to burst out of the bathroom wielding a weapon. I check just in case, then swill the juice and start to eat the banana. I normally don't like bananas, but everything is different now. I eat around the brown spots, and it actually tastes pretty good.

I wash my face, adjust my hair a little bit, and leave the room as I came, with only the clothes on my back—dark-blue jeans, an old Rolling Stones T-shirt, and a thick purple hoodie.

Our first stop is Target, and Levon seems blown away by the place, like he's just landed on another planet.

"You've never been to Target?" I ask.

"Not inside one, no."

"Where've you been hiding?"

He gives me a serious look, like that's going too far. I lead him to the girls' department where I throw some basics into the cart: underwear, socks, a blue jacket, and a bathing suit. (He did say we were going to Miami, if we make it that far.) I also get a Hello Kitty bag to put it all in. It's way too young for me, but I'm not really thinking about age-appropriate bags. We get some toiletries, a huge box of Cheez-Its, and a case of Smartwater.

"What is Smartwater?" Levon asks.

"It has electrolytes, whatever the hell that means. I just like the packaging."

"Well, I don't think you need anything to make you smarter."

He pays for it all with a wad of cash, and I avoid the eyes of the cashier, a woman with a bun on top of her head, wearing cheap, overly applied makeup. She looks like she could be a fan of the Black Angels. I hope she hasn't been watching the news. When we leave, her eyes follow me all the way out the door. When we get outside, I grab Levon and we run to the car. I get in the front.

"So, where's Cancer Stick?"

"His name is Jamal?"

"OK, where's Jamal."

"None of your business."

As we get back onto the highway, it starts to rain. Levon doesn't even slow down.

"Not so fast," I say, but it doesn't sound much like an order. I look over at him. His face has changed. It's back to being angry or indifferent. Not the same person who was looking at his girlfriend's picture last night or who actually smiled at my jokes.

"So, you don't have a cell phone either?" I ask.

"No."

"Mine is in my dorm room. Didn't get to pack for this particular excursion. But we should get one for emergencies. They have disposable pay-as-you-go ones. Don't you feel naked without one?"

Did I just say naked?

"Mine broke," he says not very convincingly.

"Anyway, I use mine mainly to surf IMDB."

"I know what that is."

"Good. There's hope yet."

He gives me a hard look. I'm pushing it again. He passes an eighteen-wheeler with pretty good precision considering the slippery conditions.

"Do you know the route without a GPS?" I ask.

"Just heading south mostly," he says. "And I got this."

He pulls out an ancient map of the states from under his seat. He shows me the page with the Eastern Seaboard, with the journey marked from Massachusetts to Florida in pen. Each stop has a colored-in circle, like a subway line.

"This is fine, but we're gonna want to avoid New York City, take the Tappan Zee Bridge. You've gone too far east."

He gives me a different look now, still surprised but also maybe a little relieved.

I scan the radio stations. It's the usual tired songs: Nickelback, Katy Perry, Kenny Chesney.

"It's always the same," I tell him. "Mainstream music is just cross-marketing. Rock sells sunglasses and leather jackets; pop sells lip gloss and soda; country sells cowboy hats and beer."

His face is momentarily unreadable. I can't tell if he's really listening or if my words are going through him.

The last station I come to, HOT 93.7, is playing "Spill It on Me."

"Well, if it isn't the song that pays for my life. And hopefully this kidnapping."

I must admit my father sounds really good on the song. He was thirty when it was recorded. Just as the third verse kicks in, Levon turns it off.

"No Butt Crack Angels for you?"

"I've heard that song one too many times."

"You and the rest of the world."

When we reach the Tappan Zee Bridge, the river underneath it shimmers, reflecting the gray clouds. Levon picks up speed again, and I check my seat belt.

"You know, the cops must be alerted. I saw a segment on the news."

"What? Did they mention me or the car?"

"I don't think so. They showed a dated picture of me, and one of my father, of course."

He slows down, checking the rearview—or what he can see out of it.

I curl my legs under myself and force myself to look out the window. It's hard not to look at him; it's like he's some sort of magnet and my eyes are made of metal.

"So what's Jamal's deal? Is he meeting up with us again?"

"Listen, leave everything to me and chill."

"Yeah, as if it's any other day?"

I don't tell him that I *am* relaxed. Something about driving and how I was raised on the road. What would I be doing right now on break in Oakland? While the Borings would be skiing in Aspen or Jackson Hole, I would be drinking coffee with Rena, maybe hanging out with Billy Ray at the train tracks. But Rena's detached mothering and Billy Ray's schoolboy crush all seem like another world to me now. The one I'm in is propelling me forward, and it's hard not to feel the rush.

Still, I need to get more of a read on Levon.

"Can you tell me one thing? How you know my father?"

He looks at me, contemplating whether to talk, then sighs and says, "My dad worked for him."

His tone is definitive, like when I asked about his girl-friend. I decide to leave it for now. Obviously my father screwed his father over in some way.

About two years ago, they did a reality show on the Black Angels, and it's been the only glimpse into my father's life

I've had since he dropped me off at Rena's house. It's so strange, watching your father on a tiny screen through the eyes of Bravo producers. Sandwiched between *Real Housewives* and *Top Chef*, the show lasted nine episodes, even though I only watched the first four. In one, the big drama was that Wade had no vegetarian food backstage at some venue in Texas. They had brought an actual pig, and he ordered them to take it away. The fat, gay chef was livid. In another, Wade had passed out on the bus, and his bandmate's teenage son drew all over him. That was kind of funny, but it all made me sick, really. I mean, didn't they ask him where his daughter was? Why do celebrities acting imperious and practicing debauchery get so praised in this country? Who even cares about the Black Angels anymore?

I start counting the dotted white lines on the highway again, like I did when I was a kid. In the seven years I toured with the band, I visited almost every state in the country—and some European countries as well. I was too young to remember much, but ironically the square-shaped states of America stick out in my mind. The flat plains stretching like a giant pancake, the red earth jutting up in ridges, the whitecaps on the streams. The world was a moving place, and my bunk on the bus was filled with stuffed animals my mom would buy me at gas stations.

STEALING CANDY

There was one—a bear wearing sunglasses—that I car-
ried with me at all times. Underneath the sunglasses, the
bear had no eyes, and that haunted my dreams. When I
asked my mother about it, she told me the bear could see
through his skin, like an octopus. I didn't know how my
mother had such strange information, but I believed her.
In fact, everything in the world, every thought I had, went
through the filter of her. To me, she knew everything.
Which is why when she died, I went back to square one: I
knew nothing at all.

The gas station we are at has stuffed animals, but no
bears with sunglasses. I grab a frog and hold it up to
Levon, giving him my best smile. I also grab some big,
black sunglasses with fake diamonds on the plastic frames.
When we get back into the car, I stick the frog on the dash
facing us. I hope it will give us good luck in whatever the
hell we are doing.

I switch on the radio again and turn it to an NPR station. There's someone reading an essay about being abused
as a child. We don't say anything for a good part of an hour.
I keep glancing over at Levon's reaction, and I can tell that
he's moved. Unlike most guys, his face doesn't reject emotion. It's almost like he can't hide it. Since I now have my
sunglasses on, he doesn't know how much I'm watching

47

him. When the woman finishes, I turn the volume down and say, "It always could be worse, I guess."

"Yeah," he says, not looking away from the road.

When I first moved to Oakland, I kept having dreams of my mother running through a field to pick me up, laughing behind a potted plant, singing that song about the wheels on the bus. The ghost of her was always there. It still is.

I look at him again and feel an urge to curl up into his arms as he drives, like in an old movie. But unfortunately, he's not Marlon Brando and we're not in a silver Thunderbird. He's a guy with a secret plan and a demonic sidekick who may return at any moment—and this crap Toyota has bucket seats.

The highway starts to slope downward into a valley, where the shivering trees huddle, lined up like frightened soldiers watching us speed by.

Levon keeps checking the rearview. Every time a car passes us from behind, he starts breathing faster.

I debate asking another question but notice Levon glaze over in a way that must have triggered a memory. Instead of asking him to elaborate, I sink into one of my own: my mother and I at the shore, somewhere in the Northwest, Oregon maybe. The clash of the mountains and the sea, the waves exploding in violent bursts. It was the first time

I had really witnessed the power of the ocean. The bus had stopped on a turnout, and some of the roadies were throwing a Frisbee. I don't remember any of the band members being there. They must have stayed on the bus.

My mother took my hand, and we walked along a path that wrapped around the mountain. As we got higher, there was more Pacific to see—a dark, inky, churning blue. We got to a bench and sat down, and my mother started rolling a cigarette. I didn't like the smell, but I loved watching her delicate fingers during the ritual and thought it was magic the way she rolled, licked, and fastened it almost all in one motion. Everything she did—walking, eating, laughing, rolling a cigarette—was fluid.

After she finished, we walked higher and higher until we couldn't see the bus at all. I started to feel scared. There was no railing, and the waves' spray was landing near our feet. She sensed my fear and held on to my hand tighter, and I closed my eyes to let the sun on my face. When I opened them, she led me to a small clearing where a few wildflowers sprouted out around some rocks. She picked one and put it in my hair. When we walked back to the bus, everyone complimented my flower, and I beamed with pride. It was a simple thing, but it went deep.

I looked up at my mother and could see her own pride

radiating off her heart-shaped face. As a child, the world revolves around you. For the first time, I could see that my mother's world revolved around me too. My father was just some guy who wore leather and screamed into a microphone, sweating under the bright, hot lights. My mother had a big, clear, open heart, but I was naive to think then that she would always keep me safe.

I must have fallen asleep, 'cause when I wake up, I see signs for Washington, DC.

"You make a noise when you sleep," Levon says.

"You mean I snore?"

"Not exactly. It's more like a whine."

"I was dreaming about my mother."

"Oh." He hands me a bottle of Smartwater.

"Be careful. I may get smart enough to run away."

"You would've done that already."

"True." I look at his expression, strong but still with a hint of vulnerability, his features blending together in some kind of beautiful accident. I sink farther into my seat.

He turns the radio to an all-news station. There are a few local stories and then an entertainment news segment. My kidnapping is the headline story, only because my father is famous, and this time a website is mentioned in addition to a tip line.

"Shit," Levon says under his breath, checking the cracked rearview again.

"We're going to have to lose the car," he says.

"And definitely change our appearance," I add. "That is, if you want to make it to Miami. These things don't go away. A legendary rock star's daughter's abduction is, like, front page. In fact, I don't even want to *see* the newspapers. The irony is that the only time I felt like anyone's daughter was when my mother was alive."

Levon checks the side mirror now, like the car that's been steadily behind us might be an unmarked cop. I hope not. I know it sounds strange, but I don't want this to end.

Chapter
7

Eventually, we pull off to a Hampton Inn on the outskirts of DC that's next to a dog adoption center. As Levon checks in, I walk over to the fence and look through. There are a bunch of pit bulls and a few mixed breeds, all in cages a little bigger than their bodies, with cement floors and dirty water bowls. I'm not sure if I've seen anything more depressing. I want to adopt them all and pile them into the back of our beat-up Toyota, but that would make us more conspicuous.

Our room smells like paint and garbage. There's a small TV, but the plug is frayed. It says in the little hotel pamphlet, which is a piece of paper folded in three, that there's a "business center." I tell Levon I'm going to see if there's an auto body place around here and also somewhere to get supplies for changing our appearance.

"That wavy hair has to go," I tell him. "I'm thinking shorter for you and blond for me."

He touches his hair and looks in the mirror, considering it.

"And I'm assuming you've got, like, a thousand for another car. Either that or we'll need a paint job, and that will run you about three hundred, I'm guessing."

"Paint job," Levon says, counting his wad of cash. "Black."

"Yes. Matte, not glossy."

I walk out, and he doesn't stop me. I could so easily turn him in, and I even think about it when the desk clerk asks, "Can I help you?"

"Yes…um, this is going to sound weird…"

"What is it, sweetheart?"

"Actually…I'm looking for the business center."

She looks at me funny, but points me to a room with faded walls and an old PC whose keys have been partially rubbed off, which makes typing a little difficult. Even so, I find an auto body shop and a Walmart, both within a five-block radius.

I check my Gmail and there are, like, a hundred new

messages in my inbox. A couple from the Borings, who suddenly care about me now. I open one of them.

> From: mathwiz555@hotmail.com
> To: candyfromastranger@gmail.com
> Subject: ?????????
>
> Candy! There are reporters all over campus—and camera crews. They checked your laptop and went through your books and stuff. We didn't know your dad was famous. Is that what this is about? They keep asking us all these questions. We told them that you keep to yourself and like to make your films. I hope you are OK.
>
> Your friend,
> Brittany

Friend? That's a stretch. I wonder if my popularity will go up now that I've been kidnapped. Even though the Borings are boring, being with them did feel like a community or whatever. There was stuff that we sometimes did together without having to interact. Watch a movie or study. Speaking of studying, I hope Brittany turned in our report for social studies. It was the only assignment I still had to turn in before break. Did she really not know who my father is? There was a mention of me going to NRS in *Us Weekly*, but who reads that anyway? Well, I do, but only when I'm bored out of my skull at the dentist's office or sitting at the barbershop near campus where the only choice is that or *Field and Stream*.

The only person I want to reach out to is Fin, but I don't think he does email. Neither does my grandmother. The rest of the emails are from teachers and other people from the school, but I see one in the middle that stands out. It's Billy Ray, who I haven't heard from in a while.

From: tapwaterrocks@yahoo.com
To: candyfromastranger@gmail.com
Subject: Holy shit

Candy Cane—

I saw you on the news this a.m., wtf? It was weird, cause I've been thinking about you a lot. Tap Water broke up, and I'm

doing solo stuff now. You would totally
hate it. I miss you. Please don't be dead.

Billy Ray

I am close to hitting Reply, but I realize that the police
could monitor my emails from the IP address. In fact, I
better shut down now, in case they already have.

On my way back, I duck into the lobby bathroom and
film myself again.

"Candy Rex, in the flesh. I'm now in DC. I don't think
the guy I'm with is going to hurt me. But his partner,
Jamal, already did. If something happens and I die, please
tell Rena thanks for taking me in, even though she's never
hugged me and her house smells like mothballs…and please
give my royalties to Fin Adams, the janitor at NRS, and tell
my father, Wade Rex, he's an asshole."

When I get back to the room, Levon is looking at the
pictures from his wallet again. His lips rest in that half smile,
like he's dreaming of a better place.

"There's an auto body shop that will paint the car a few
blocks away and a Walmart," I say.

"Cool," he says, still looking at the pictures.

I'm not sure how long I stand there gazing at him

before a piercing siren in the parking lot snaps me out of my trance. Levon springs up and grabs my arm, leads me into the bathroom, and says, "Shh… Just be quiet."

I look around the bathroom. It's depressing but also familiar—I grew up in hotel bathrooms. I have a sinking feeling that he's going to be caught, that all of this is going to end. Was it 'cause I checked my email? I think of the red car, sitting out there like a giant zit in the face of the parking lot. We should have ditched it sooner.

Please, please. Don't catch us now.

Chapter 8

The sirens continue, and my heart goes into triple time. I am panting like a crazed animal. Twenty seconds feel like an eternity, until Levon finally opens the door to the bathroom.

"Stay there. Don't move."

He slams the door, which startles me.

Does this have something to do with Jamal? Did the police catch him, and he led them to us?

I wait, wondering what would happen if this *did* end. Back to my regular life? Is it really as bad as I think? I stare down at my hands, which are shaking slightly.

Levon comes back into the bathroom and sits down on the floor.

He is holding a gun.

"Is that real?"

"No, it's a fucking water pistol. What do you think?"

He's really angry now, and I realize how stupid I've been to think that he actually cares about my well-being. He looks at me, an entire past fleeting in the light behind his eyes, a whole life I know nothing about.

The sirens stop, and he goes back into the room. Through the crack in the door, I see him looking out the window, the gun still in his hand.

"Levon," I call out.

"Shut up, Candy!" he whispers really loud.

I shut the door and sit back on the closed toilet. It must have been my email. They must have tracked us.

I'm not sure how long it is before he opens the door and says, "You can come out. It was an ambulance."

I walk out into the room and peek out the cloudy window. The ambulance is leaving. Two uniformed men get out of an official-looking van and let out what look like more pit bulls for the shelter.

I walk over to the cheap mirror and pretend to examine my face, but I'm really watching Levon, sitting on the bed, looking cold and distant, and it occurs to me once again that this all could be a bad idea.

"Do your parents know where you are?" I ask him casually.

"Can you just shut up? For real, Candy. I need to think."

"OK, OK."

We sit in silence for a while, until there's a knock on the door. Levon walks toward it, the gun still in his hand. I hide between the bed and the wall.

"Yeah?" Levon asks through the closed door.

"Sorry, wrong room," I hear someone say.

We sit in silence some more, and he turns to me, apparently ready to answer the question.

"My mom is in Texas, haven't seen her since I was a kid. My dad…"

Say it, Levon, just say it.

"My dad's in jail."

"Oh."

Even though he's spooked, his eyes still shine.

"Insurance fraud?"

He lets out his small bark of a nervous laugh. "No."

"Nothing violent though, right?"

He puts his hands together, tips of his fingers touching. "It's complicated," he says, which is code for *I can't really tell you.*

"Complicated how?"

"He's not a violent person. I mean, he loses his temper like everyone else, but...he's innocent."

"He didn't do this thing, this...sort of violent thing?"

"No."

"And I'm assuming that's why we're here?"

He nods.

I breathe in, hold it, and then breathe out slowly.

What did my dad do? If Levon's father loses his temper and wound up in jail, what does that make Levon? I need to get a cell phone. Now.

"OK, well, before any more sirens, we need to do something about the car," I say.

He nods again, and we start to get ready.

Twenty minutes later, we're in a tiny office in the back of an auto body shop, flanked by a dirty, red throw rug and two worn leather chairs. The owner, a one-armed guy named Eel, says his "boys" will paint the car black for $350. He doesn't seem suspicious at all—I'm sure he's seen it all.

"Where did his arm go? Was it a *Fargo* moment?" I whisper to Levon, who tries not to smile. As he starts to hand Eel the money, I stop him, pretending I'm his girlfriend.

"Babe, I need my hair done. I was going to get highlights, the kind you like."

He looks at me, incredulous.

"Three hundred cash," I say to Eel. "Final offer."

"Deal," he says, like it's nothing. I probably could've gotten him down to two fifty, but Levon seems impressed by the fifty-dollar discount. *What else can I impress him with?*

We go to a trendy burger place, and the menu is written on this huge chalkboard above the cashier station. I imagine someone running a wet cloth down the center of it, obliterating someone's meticulous work. All the rules suddenly erased. We stare at the lists of choices—over a hundred of them.

"What happened to lettuce and tomato?" Levon asks.

"Get the one with bacon and blue cheese," I tell him.

"OK."

"I'm getting the California—avocado and ranch."

We eat our burgers while Eel and his boys paint our car. It feels like I'm still a character in someone else's movie and something bad is eventually going to happen, but right now I'm in the sweet spot, on a road to nowhere. The burger tastes amazing.

"Did you know food tastes better when you're happy?"

"I guess," he says, looking at me funny.

Levon cuts his burger in half and puts mustard on his fries. He wipes his mouth after every bite.

I notice someone staring at us from the corner of the restaurant and check if there's anything behind me—just a wall.

"We've got a peeping Tom at four o'clock," I tell him. "I'll meet you at Walmart." Levon gives me an extremely slight nod, and I slip out the side door.

Outside, the afternoon sun is burning its last light, evening threatening. It's a seedy part of DC, but the buildings seem to glow in the muted dusk. I think about my picture on the TV and secretly smile. It feels good to be wanted. We are outlaws, Levon and me. As I walk, my happiness is darkened by a pang of fear about Jamal—lurking in my thoughts like a snake, ready to bite. *Is he coming back?*

Phone, phone. Even though she's completely unemotional, Rena does care about me. She must be worried. I really need to call her. And Fin. I need him to get my films.

I stand outside Walmart, trying to block out the feeling of Jamal's fist, the look in his fierce eyes, his dirty smirk while he sat on the cot. I check around for cops or any official-looking vehicles.

I could just keep walking. People will know who I am, anyone who watches the news. But I don't want to. I know it's stupid, but I have to follow through with this.

Walmart is packed with people in ten-dollar T-shirts

with dirt under their fingernails, curses piercing their sentences like stains.

I meet up with Levon near the pharmacy section.

"Who was that guy?" I ask.

"It's cool. He stopped staring after you left."

"That's what I'm worried about. It's me on the news, not you."

"Let's do this fast and get back," he says.

I get scissors for his hair and dye for mine. I also get him a cowboy hat, which he tells me he'll never wear. It's a no-cattle hat, popular with white girls on spring break. Either way, it's only seven dollars, so it goes in the cart. In electronics, I show him the pay-as-you-go cell phone for forty bucks, with twenty-five anytime minutes on it.

"We can't travel without a phone. It's an absolute necessity."

We pay and walk quickly back to the auto body shop, trying not to be conspicuous. If I were writing the script, Levon would be my boyfriend, and we would drive off, starting some rebel life together. But no, we're going to Miami so he can…what? Try to blackmail my loser dad who probably won't give him a dime? What will happen to us then? I grab his hand, and he looks at me like I'm crazy, shaking it off.

"C'mon. The car's probably done."

He's right. It's not the greatest paint job, but the Toyota just went from a literal red flag to a more under-the-radar heap of black junk. I actually like it.

"This reads kidnapping way less," I say, getting in with our Walmart bags.

"Shh," Levon says. Eel is standing right next to the car. Even if he did hear us, it's not like he watches the news.

When we get back to our gritty room, we start the disguising process. I figure we need a sound track, so I tune the cheap radio to some auto-tuned hip-hop track. I cut Levon's hair under the light from the dusty lamp between the beds, using a thin, white towel to catch the scraps.

Came up that's all me.

He looks even better with short hair. His eyes expand, or at last seem bigger, and his lips take more prominence on his face, upstaging even those rigid cheekbones. There's a fluttering inside me, like a buzzing insect, a tiny ball of frenetic energy that I pray is not showing on my face. The song builds.

No help, that's all me, all me for real.

He shakes off the excess hair and glances at himself in the streaked mirror. He seems apathetic. It strikes me that vanity is not high on his list.

"Looks good," I say, even though it looks way more than good. The guy is the literal definition of *hot*.

He heads into the bathroom, and I listen to the sounds he makes, picturing him in there. When he comes out and I go in, our arms brush against each other, and I'm hyper-aware of it. He doesn't seem to notice.

"Your turn," he says.

While I'm in the bathroom dying my hair, Levon steps out, and I wait for the dye to do its work. He comes back with a pint of whiskey, which he pours into two paper cups.

"How'd you get that?"

"The lady didn't card me."

I try not to give away how impressed I am.

My roots start to burn a little, but I don't care. When I really think about it, this could be the best thing that's ever happened to me. I grab one of the cups of whiskey, and Levon says, "You're welcome."

After I rinse my hair, I'm surprised by how good it looks. I wanted to go for white-trash runaway, but it sort of looks authentic—like I actually could have a name like Bree or Madison. When I come out and look at Levon for the second time, I realize his haircut not only passes for an actual one, but also makes him look even more mysterious. I try to hide my surprise, but it's not working because he says, "What?"

"Nothing."

We turn on the news, and at first I'm relieved there's no mention of us. But when they tease our story before the commercial break, my heart picks up again.

"It's good we painted the car, trust me," I tell him. "And we both look totally different. No one's going to recognize us, if we're careful," I say.

He downs his whiskey and nods. I pour another for both of us. I don't drink much, but whiskey is my choice when I do.

"What about the license plate?"

"We used a different one," he says. "The one we have now is legit."

"Wow," I say.

"One thing Jamal was good for."

I flash again to Jamal on the cot, his searing eyes. At least he mentioned Jamal in the past tense. Maybe he's gone for good.

The news comes back on, and my name is on the scroll at the bottom. I wonder if Rena's watching the same news we are all the way across the country.

"Can I call my grandmother real quick?"

He seems skeptical.

"It's just to tell her I'm fine. I'll hang up in less than

twenty-two seconds, which is how long it takes to trace a call. Not that they even know what phone we're using."

He stares at me for a second. "OK, but no funny business."

I giggle at his dated phrase and dial, grateful that I know her number by heart.

Rena answers on the fourth ring. She's not hysterical like a typical grandmother receiving a call from her kidnapped granddaughter. Still, there is urgency in her voice.

"Candy. Where are you? Is some joke?"

"No, Rena, but I'm fine. I'm not"—I peer over at Levon, sipping his whiskey with his new boyish haircut—"in danger."

"Where are you? Tell me, Candy."

"I'm…somewhere near New York," I say, which is not exactly a lie.

"There are reporters. They here twenty-five seven."

Typical that she would get the phrase wrong. One could call her broken English charming, if one could ever describe Rena as charming.

"Don't tell them anything. This is really important, Rena. Don't tell them you talked to me. Just know that I'm OK. This will all be over within a week or so."

The thought makes my heart dip, like when you reach the peak on a Ferris wheel. I hang up as she mumbles something in Russian. The phone rings back, but Levon grabs it and turns it off—or at least tries to—but I end up helping him. I guess I won't be calling Fin, although I don't have his number. I'm sure he's trying to find me. He's always looked after me. One time, when some seniors were taunting me, he drove his lawn mower right at them. I laughed as the boys scattered.

After the commercial break, my father's face comes on the screen, and it's like watching a soap opera. He is in faux-worry mode, acting like his world is crumbling. I want something to throw at the TV. There is nothing—the cheap clock is screwed into the table.

"Oh my God!" I yell.

"What?" Levon asks.

"Like he cares! I haven't seen him in years."

After a minute, the same picture of me comes on the screen—my junior picture from NRS. Levon laughs, and this time I tell *him* to shut up.

"That's me, a thirty-second segment," I say as they cut to another story. "At least it was at the top of the hour."

Levon smiles, but then in a flash, his face goes stern. "Candy, he's still your father."

"Yeah? Funny how you're sticking up for him after kidnapping his daughter."

That shuts him up.

Chapter 9

We are past Richmond and almost coming into Raleigh when we see our first real cop. He's parked on the median about three hundred yards ahead. I immediately lean over, laying my head on Levon's lap and thinking that this could be a totally different situation. After we go through the underpass, I sit up and look back, then over at Levon. He's chewing the inside of his lip.

"Did he look at you?"

"Yes, he's coming," Levon says. "Fuck!"

He starts breathing heavy. The cop gets closer, and I can feel my heart in my temples.

"We aren't speeding," I tell him.

"I know!" he yells, clearly freaking out.

"Put on your blinker and get off at the next exit."

The cop is right behind us. I close my eyes tight, like a kid watching a horror movie. When I open them, the cop is still there.

"Drive normally."

"I am, Candy!"

"OK, OK."

We change lanes and the cop does too, continuing to trail us.

"God dammit," Levon says.

"Just—"

"Don't talk, Candy. Shut up, please."

"OK, but you're doing fine."

He slams his hands against the wheel.

For the next two miles, the cop remains a steady car length behind us. I keep waiting to hear a siren or see the lights. But nothing. Only Levon, breathing heavy and tapping his fingers really fast.

Finally, the siren sounds, and the lights spin, but he's passing us, pulling someone else over.

We don't say anything, continuing to drive in silence.

Levon's breathing returns to normal, and he's not

tapping his fingers anymore, but he's still obsessively checking the mirrors.

"Good thing we painted the car and did our hair," I say.

He's really serious now, like a whole other person. He
nods, but he seems super spooked, like a kid who just woke
up from a nightmare in a dark house with no parents.

For the next hour, it's just the sound of the wheels and
our own thoughts. I go through my list again. *Gone Baby
Gone. Saw.* Both girls, but only one survived. I crack the
window, and the whizzing sound reminds me of my years
on the tour bus. The trouble with moving is that the road
never goes on forever.

I pull down the sun visor, which has a tiny mirror on it,
and look at myself. My hair still looks strange to me, but it
also kind of works. I'm a brunette now stuck in the body
of a blond.

"I would never want to be blond all the time. People
assume you're dumb."

Levon makes a face. "What about Hillary Clinton?"

"Yeah, but she's, like, sixty. If you're young and blond,
you're ditzy—even the smart ones."

"I assume you mean the girls at your school?"

"Yes, but back in Oakland too."

"Is it true what you said?" he asks in his new serious tone.

"What?"

"You haven't seen Wade in years?"

"Yes. Even when he comes to play the same city I'm in, he doesn't come to see me. Heartwarming, huh?"

"Wow..."

"It's cool. I'm used to it. Actually, I only have one memory of hanging out and having fun with him. Isn't that weird?"

"At least you have one."

"You sure know how to look on the bright side, don't you?"

"I grew up in a trailer," he says, tilting his head and glancing at me out of the corner of his eye. "That shit was not the Berkshires."

"Believe me, NRS is not a postcard once you walk inside. I mean, my school is good, but I just don't feel like I really belong there."

"Where do you belong?"

On a highway with you, I think. *Maybe.*

"I don't know. I want to make films. I've made a couple."

"Cool."

"Ever since I was given my first video camera at age nine, I've been shooting and editing films. It's nice to document stuff, to know that life isn't so fleeting. When I see paintings or photographs, they look so one-dimensional. I want to step inside the frame and make them come alive."

He nods, glancing in the side mirror. "I watch a lot. Films, I mean."

"So, are you going to tell me why your dad was in jail?"

He checks the cracked rearview yet again, maybe this time to make sure the past is behind him. "Not now. Tell me about the one fun time you mentioned, with your dad."

I put my feet up on the seat and hug my knees close, and Levon turns the radio down.

"It was a few months before my mother died, actually. I was seven. We were at Joshua Tree. Do you know it?"

"California?"

"Yes. It's this vast landscape of nothing except for a couple trees that sprout over the horizon. They kind of look like giant flowers. I'm sure you've seen pictures. Anyway, there was an eighteen-wheeler that had an accident, and after they had cleared the wreckage, there were all these cans of whipped cream that had rolled off the truck that had been carrying them. Hundreds and hundreds of them, dotting the fields, everywhere. It was early morning, and the sky was surreal, almost purple. My dad woke me up, and I remember wondering if I was still dreaming—maybe I was. Anyway, we went outside and drew this huge peace sign out of whipped cream, in the field in front of Joshua Tree. It was the coolest thing in the world for a seven-year-old."

"The coolest whip you mean?"

"Ha. Anyway, as we were walking back to the bus, he sprayed my head from a can he'd saved. I tried to eat it, then I rubbed some on him, and we were laughing so hard. It was the only time I'd really seen him laugh. He always smiled his dumb, stage smile, but that day, it was like he wasn't a rock star. We were just kids playing with whipped cream."

A silence comes over the car. Levon looks straight ahead as the white dashes come at us, then disappear under the hood in a flash. He's watching the road, but something beyond it too, something out of his grasp.

"What are you looking for?" I ask him.

He thinks for a minute and then says, "Retribution, I guess."

"For your dad?"

"Yes."

"How long has he been in jail?"

"Two years."

He turns the radio back up, so I figure that's all I'm going to get for now. It's a college station, probably out of Durham. I can tell 'cause the DJ is meek and the songs are obscure. You would never hear a ten-minute Led Zeppelin B-side on mainstream radio. I pull out my handheld and check what's on there. The footage I took while I was bound is of the backseat, then the motel people, the help number on the TV, Levon with his shirt off, and my confessions. At the very beginning, it's just Fin's dog trying to destroy an old sock. Seeing that feels like it was a different life. Pre-abduction. Will I see everything that way now? Before and after?

"Don't turn that camera on me," Levon says.

"Incriminating evidence?"

"Yeah that, but also I don't like cameras, never have."

"Why? You're totally photogenic."

He scoffs, but red blotches appear at the top of his cheeks.

We pull over at a sad gas station with a small convenience store. I can see the guy behind the counter, black hair with a streak of purple, an eyebrow ring, and a smattering of acne on his chin.

It could be worse. I could be working here, the stench of gasoline and all those dusty chocolate bars staring at me all day.

Levon comes back with a bag of pretzels and two Sprites. As we get back on the highway, we start in on the pretzels. They are dry and too salty, but once again, something feels right. I know that, inevitably, our time together will be over soon. But that doesn't mean I don't wish that Miami were ten thousand miles away.

Eventually we pull into a Comfort Inn parking lot that looks deserted. He tells me to wait in the car, and just in case, I turn the handheld on myself and make another recording.

"Me again. I'm at a Comfort Inn somewhere in North Carolina. My kidnapper is named Levon, and his father worked for my father."

I turn the camera toward the lobby and film Levon as he's walking out of the hotel, putting it away before he catches me.

Chapter

10

Our room tonight is definitely an upgrade. There are mints on the pillows, the rug smells new, and the toilet paper has been curled back into a flower shape, which makes me think of my mother. She didn't smell bad, but she was kind of a hippie. She never wore leather or teased her hair. She would put flower petals all over the bus, and sometimes my father would wake up with one stuck to his forehead. It made him look even more ridiculous then he already did.

He always wore tight pants and shirts that seemed like they'd look better on tween girls. He rarely ate, and you could usually see his rib cage. When he spoke, he mostly mumbled. Still, girls lined up by the hundreds for a glimpse of him. I became immune to it: the screaming, the photographers, watching him autograph body parts. There was something he had onstage though—charisma, I guess—and maybe he still does. But to me it always looked like spastic dance moves and dramatic hair flips. And even though his voice has been called one of the best in rock and roll, I never remember him singing to me.

Levon does push-ups while I take a hot bath and read the local newspaper they left on our little desk. Thankfully, there's nothing about us. But in the entertainment section, there's a review of the Black Angels show that came through Raleigh. The headline reads, "Wade Rex Has Still Got It."

Yeah, a daughter, I think.

I scan down to the last paragraph, which is always the most important in a review.

> As the last note of "Spill It on Me" rang out in feedback, some of the middle-aged moms tried to beat the crowds out of the arena. Yes, they had to save that song for last, but could you blame them? With bands twenty years their juniors on the rise, the Black Angels have stood the test of time, even if Wade Rex,

sweat dripping his guy-liner down
his cheeks, looked like some kind of
deranged Rock God, raising his ema-
ciated arms like he was praying. For
what? We can only imagine...

Deranged Rock God. Yep. That pretty much explains it.

When I get back into the room, Levon is sitting on the bed holding my HD mini handheld. He looks at me and slowly shakes his head. He must have found it under my pillow.

"I-I just did it as a precaution."

"So, what, you're an act? All of this is an act?"

"All of what, Levon?"

"Look, I didn't go to a school like yours, but I'm not stupid. I erased over the parts where you said my name and where you filmed me."

I sit down slowly on the bed across from him.

"I didn't do that for evidence. It was more for Jamal."

"Yeah, right. How am I supposed to trust you now?"

"How am I supposed to trust you?" I yell, not even knowing where the fuel for my emotion is coming from. It's like someone pushed my freak-out button. "You fuck-ing let that guy strangle me and punch me in the head!"

"Candy, you wouldn't stop talking. Now please, let's stop talking."

I lie down and stare at the ceiling, which has tiny sparkles in it. I imagine them as stars, and I wish on each one that blinks that I didn't mess everything up.

He calls and orders a pizza, and I almost tell him extra cheese, but I stay quiet. He tells them his name is Frank. In spite of everything, his harmless lie makes me smile.

Twenty minutes later, a punk kid comes to the door with the delivery.

"Frank?"

"Yeah," Levon says, handing him cash.

The kid's got metal piercings all over his face and neon-orange hair. He looks over Levon's shoulder at me. I could give him a sign. I could run out the door, but I don't.

Levon takes a slice for himself and drops the box on my bed.

It's not the greatest pizza, but it tastes OK because I'm starving.

After he finishes his first slice, he grabs another one and sits on my bed.

"No more filming anything that might be used as evidence." His voice is lower than usual, like his demand must be taken seriously. I wait for him to smile or something—or give me some kind of assurance—but he doesn't. He just stares at me evenly.

"OK," I say, trying to keep my face like his, a blank slate.

"How do I know you won't run off now? How do I know you weren't planning to all along?"

"'Cause I didn't."

"If you do anything else, I'll have to detain you."

Where did he hear that, a bad cop show?

I want so badly to believe that he's putting on a tough guy act, that it's not who he really is, but I can't be sure.

Chapter 11

A long succession of highway lines under a blinding sun.

I put my hoodie up 'cause it feels more fugitive and roll the window down a little. The air is definitely not as cold as Massachusetts, but it still has a bite. A few miles down the interstate, we pass a sign for Cape Fear.

The moment I read the word *Fear*, I hear it.

The high-pitched shrills of a truncated police siren. This time the cop is not following us; he's pulling us over.

Levon slows and turns into the breakdown lane carefully. He sighs and tells me to stay quiet. I pull my hoodie down and turn to look at the flashing lights behind us. My heart is a drum, thumping inside my rib cage, reverberating through my whole body. I look at Levon's brow, which is glistening with sweat. I tell myself that only our age and our sex are traceable. The car, our hair, everything is different.

Breathe.

The cop is more than six feet tall, wearing a thick belt and a shiny pistol in a holster. He peers in, looking a little suspicious, and I try to give him a casual smile, even though he can probably hear my heart beating.

Levon hands him his license and the registration, which is actually in his own name, and the cop goes back to his car. I look over, expecting Levon to be freaking out as much as I am, but he actually seems calm.

"Don't worry," he says. "I changed lanes without signaling." His shaky tone belies his nonchalance.

"Yeah, that must be it, not kidnapping."

He grabs my hand and squeezes it. I notice his forearm again, the faint brown hair in a perfect pattern.

"Candy. If we act like nothing is out of the ordinary, he won't think anything is."

"The registration. It will say the car's red."

"Shit…" Levon squints his eyes and starts chewing the inside of his lip again.

"Maybe he'll only look at the expiration. And the plates."

He's still holding my hand. I close my eyes, willing him to keep it there. When I open them again, I see the cop approaching in the side rearview mirror. His stride is lazy, like it's just another routine traffic stop. I'm praying the guy's not listening to his APBs.

"What brings you to North Carolina?" the cop asks as he hands the license and registration back to Levon, who hands it to me. The cop looks at him, then at me, then back at him. The moment stretches on like someone pulling a rubber band slowly until it threatens to snap. The silence is too much for me to bear. Levon obviously doesn't have an answer, and I switch into damage-control mode.

"I'm in film studies, and I'm doing a project for school. We're going to see the town of Cape Fear."

The words seem to come out independent of my brain. The cop looks like the type of guy who probably plays catch with his son and mows the lawn every Sunday. He's a regular person, and we are too—for the most part. What signs are there for him to think otherwise? I put my hands underneath my thighs and give him another smile.

"Ah. Well, you've passed the exit. But if you take 87 South and then a left at Gray's Creek, you should be good. In the meantime, I'll give you a verbal warning. Your speed was in check, but remember to use that turn signal for changing lanes. That's what it's there for. Also, you need to get that rearview fixed. There's a place in Cape Fear called Dixie Automotive. They'll pop another on there for you."

"Thanks, Officer, I will. I'll do that," Levon says a little too earnestly.

"Good luck on your project, young lady." He tips his hat and smiles at me, then heads back toward his car.

Levon and I stare at each other, our eyes bulging.

The show must go on.

"Thanks for that," Levon says as we pull back into the lane.

"It was nothing," I tell him, acting like I had planned it that way.

For the next few miles, we watch the rearview but don't see the cop anywhere.

"So who's Billy Ray?" Levon asks.

"What?"

"You said his name in your sleep."

My face flushes with a wave of anxiety.

"He's a friend from Oakland."

"Your boyfriend?"

"Not really."

"I see." Levon holds back a smile.

I change the subject. "We have to go to Cape Fear now, in case the cop trails us. We can't look conspicuous."

"Definitely. Unless he figures out who we are and comes after us."

"I don't think we have to worry about that guy."

The cop's directions are spot-on. When we pull into the main part of town, I can picture the location scouts coming here and thinking, *yes*. It's quaint enough on the surface, but you can tell there are secrets lurking in the corners. Plus, it actually *looks* like a movie set. There are town houses in different colors with flower boxes and old-fashioned streetlights. Boats dot the glassy harbor, and birds soar leisurely in V formations. For a second, I imagine us staying here and starting a life.

We park and go to the College Diner where the red vinyl booths have rips in them, the insides threatening to burst out. The place is empty except for a family, a couple sailors, and a woman in a tracksuit drinking coffee at the counter. Her coffee mug has lipstick smudges all around the rim, as if she rotated it for each sip. When Levon notices me dumping three sugar packets into my iced tea, he looks away like he's seen something he shouldn't.

We order "smothered chicken," because it seems to be what everyone's having. But we're not everyone. We are on the run, and we are on a mission. We don't talk much during lunch, still processing the close call we got out of by some miracle. Everything seems to have settled—until the end of our meal when our story runs on the flat-screen TV, the one modern appliance in the whole place. There's no sound, but I can see the same picture of me, and this time they show an exterior shot of NRS and an old logo from the Black Angels. Clearly it's a local channel. We pay the check and leave discreetly, not talking again until we're back on the highway.

"No lane changing without a signal," I say.

"Got it."

I lean against the window and close my eyes, hoping my mother was right, that the road really is a chance. A chance for what? I don't know. But something is better than nothing, and the fact that tomorrow is a blank canvas on which anything could be painted is both scary and thrilling.

~

I dream that someone is leading me through a forest of pines. I am watching my bare feet crunching the pine needles. The ground is moist, and so is the air. We move through pockets of fog until we come to a ridge overlooking a deep gully. I look up into the face of the person leading me. It's Levon, and he's smiling...

I wake with only my eyes, not moving my body so he thinks I'm still asleep. I still have sunglasses on, so again he doesn't know I'm watching him. He is mouthing along to the words of a Maroon 5 song and tilting his head a little on the beat. The scruff on his face is a little more pronounced in the afternoon light, and though he keeps checking the mirrors, he seems happy-go-lucky, like he's just on a road trip with a friend. It's kind of how I feel too, even if he might be leading me off a cliff. I stare at his full lips, and I imagine that instead of the dumb pop lyrics, he's saying my name and telling me I'm beautiful, that he wants to take me away. That the fall from the cliff is actually what we need.

We drive until dark, then pull into a Super 8 in the city of Florence off I-95, one of the marks on the old map Levon has. In our now-usual routine, he checks us in, and I meet him at the room. I wince when I enter. The place should really be called a Super 2. There are stains on the rugs, the wallpaper's peeling, and the tub has faded from white to a sickly brown. It smells like a cross between an ashtray and a locker room. The sign read, "From $39," and now I see why.

Levon says he's going for a run and tells me he'll be back in about twenty minutes.

"You don't think I'm going to leave?"

"You said it yourself. You would have already. But don't even think about changing your mind. Keep this door locked."

"I will."

He believes me, but when he leaves, I stare at the door. *Where would I go? To the police? What would that mean for Levon?* In a way I can't really pinpoint, I want to stay. It's not logical, just what I feel. Like I'm finally awake.

I turn on the news, and our story is still there. I am looking at the same picture of myself, which I'm used to now. I actually laugh a little. The whole world has no idea what's really happening. There's a shot of Rena closing the door on reporters, and I think, *Good for you.*

There's a knock at the door and figure it must be Levon, who left his key or something. Just to be safe, I slide the cover of the peep hole to double-check.

It's not Levon. It's a dark-skinned man in worn jeans and a black windbreaker, carrying something behind his back. His eyes are staring at the door, pupils shaking.

Chapter 12

I jump back from the door.

Jamal?

As I sink down with my back against the sidewall, he knocks again, this time harder. My throat is a vise grip, not letting air in or out. I instinctively look around the room, wondering if there's anything I could use as a weapon.

How the hell did he find us? Was he meant to come back? Was he the one who marked the route on the map?

"I know someone's in there," I hear him say, his voice hoarse and dry. "I saw you. Open up, or I'm breaking in."

I can feel sweat forming on my brow and wipe it with my sleeve.

How can this be happening? We are hundreds of miles from where he last left us. Was that what his expression meant while sitting on the cot? That he'd be back? Was he following us all along? Does Levon know?

I look at the phone on the table between the beds. I could use it, but who would I call? 911? Levon would be screwed. Jamal has seen the car outside, even though it's black now. He knows we're here.

Please, Levon, come back.

I put my ear up to the door and can hear Jamal's erratic breathing through it.

"What do you want? We don't have drugs."

He bangs on the door with enough force that I leap back and fall on the floor.

"Levon!"

"He's not here!"

I realize that he probably wants money. But Levon's not stupid; he has his cash on him. So I'm not going to be able to get rid of Jamal. I have to stall him.

He bangs again.

"Open up! Now!"

I hear myself moan. I wonder how easy it would be for

him to break down the decrepit door. Definitely faster than 911 would get here. I notice the lamp on the side table. It's seventies style, in the shape of a teardrop, and it's not screwed to the table. I crawl over and unplug it, my hands shaking as I pull off the shade and unscrew the lightbulb. It is made of wood, and thankfully it's solid. If he breaks down the door, it's my only chance. I hold it by the skinny end and crouch in the corner.

"Open the fucking door, or I'll kill you." Jamal says, this time almost tenderly. He's not bluffing.

Then I hear another door open, and a man's voice, a little slurred.

"Would you mind keeping it down?" the man says.

I don't hear Jamal respond, but the door moves slightly, so I imagine he sat down. I have to remind myself to take each breath. This is not Netflix. I can't think of what Chloë Grace Moretz or Angelina Jolie would do—it's all up to me. I'm the leading lady, but there is no script.

I can smell smoke from Jamal's cigarette coming under the door. I can hear him blowing out his drags sharply.

Where the hell is Levon? He's been gone almost an hour.

"Leave us alone," I say through the closed door.

Jamal gets up and it seems like he's walking away, but then I hear a loud *boom*.

Jamal's throwing himself into the door, hoping to knock it down.

Was his plan to kidnap me from Levon? Get more money?

BA-BOOM.

"Hey, buddy." The man from next door is back. "Whoever's in there is not letting you in. Can you keep it down? I got a baby."

"Why the hell you bring a baby to a shithole like this?" Jamal asks him.

"Whoa," the guy says. "Easy."

Then I hear a door close quietly.

Did Jamal pull a weapon on him? How psycho is Jamal really?

Right then, my whole body reverts into some kind of crazy survival-tactic supercharge. I pull the end table and wedge it into the corner that the door opens into. I stand on the table so that my head brushes the ceiling, the lamp in my good arm. I slowly extend my left foot, pushing the door lever down slowly.

"OK, OK," I say.

Jamal walks into the room without seeing me. I pinpoint the top of his head, and like I'm smashing an insect, I thrust the lamp forward. The sound resonates after the lamp hits his skull, which is way harder that I thought it was.

He collapses, faceup, eyes rolled into the back of his head.

I run into the bathroom, lock the door, and sit on the edge of the tub. Breathing is now even harder. I think I'm hyperventilating. Tears rush off my eyelids.

Please come back, Levon. Please.

My arm is still reverberating pins and needles. I grab some tissue and clean off my face.

I'm not sure how long it is—a minute or two?—until I start to rock, which I haven't done since I was a little girl. But it helps. Then I hum one of the songs my mother used to sing to me. The one about the foolish frog.

I have to do something. What if Levon doesn't come back? I open the bathroom door a crack. Jamal is still on the floor. I make a run for it, but he grabs my leg and I scream. He is conscious again.

I look around for something, a weapon, anything.

Jamal gets up and stands between me and the door, breathing irregularly and staring at me with unconcealed rage. He slowly takes the Toyota keys from the table.

"Leave us alone," I say weakly. "Just take his money."

"You, crazy bitch, you are worth way more than what he has."

For a second I think he's going to hug me, but he hoists me on his shoulder. I try to wriggle free, but I'm in some sort of death grip. He carries me outside, shoves me in the trunk of the Toyota, and slams the door while I'm still screaming, hoping someone will hear. But then there's nothing. Silence, and everything goes dark. I hear him get in, start the car, and peel out, and my head bangs on an old rusty jack.

"Levon," I say pathetically. "Levon."

I'm in a trunk, my head is throbbing, fumes are burning my nostrils, and I'm thinking about Levon. *Is he OK? Why was he gone so long?* The car is on the highway now, and I'm trying not to cry, but it's not working. I start thinking of all the bad things I've done to deserve this, but it doesn't really add up. Stealing batteries, skipping class, writing my name to check in for study hour but then leaving. I'm locked in a trunk, and I might die of asphyxiation or shock or trauma. I'm being driven around by a crazed meth head, and this is not fun anymore. This is actually the worst thing that's ever happened to me. How stupid am I to not have left when I had the chance? I don't know how to pray, so I just keep whispering the word *please* over and over.

I manage to shift my body so that I'm breathing fewer fumes. My head is still throbbing, but it's more of a dull ache. I start to doze off, and at first I fight it, because I know I'm not supposed to sleep after hitting my head, but it's no use. I'm gone.

Eventually I snap awake to someone slipping a key into the trunk to unlock it. As soon as it opens, I flip into super-charge survival mode again and kick the roof of the trunk as hard as I can. Jamal yells, and his body falls back. Then I hear what sounds like a crack, then nothing. I peek out of the trunk. We're in the parking lot of a roadside bar, and there are only a few other cars there. No people.

I get out of the trunk and stand there in shock. Time slows, and I feel dizzy. Then my eyes come into focus and I see someone running toward me, saying my name.

It's Levon.

He crouches over Jamal, his mouth completely slack.

"He said he was going to kill me," I say, 'cause it's true.

Jamal's head has hit a rock and blood is spilling out of it, making a dark pool in the dirt. We both stand there, watching the pool slowly get bigger. I don't want Levon to see, but more tears start to pour out of my eyes.

"Are you OK?"

"Yes."

"OK. Help me. We have to move him."

We each grab a wrist and drag him behind an old, decaying fence, next to an abandoned pickup truck. In the back, there's a tarp. Levon throws it over Jamal, but it barely does the job.

The keys, which Jamal was holding, are sitting in the pool of blood. Levon grabs them, wipes them on his jeans, and tells me to get in the car.

"Wait. We can't leave him there."

Levon looks at me, incredulous.

"Are you serious?"

I wipe the dried tears on my cheek with my sleeve. I don't know what is overtaking me or if I'm even in my right mind, but I know we need to do something about this.

"Let's take him to a hospital and drop him off."

"There are security cameras—"

"Levon! We can't just leave a person to die!"

He looks at me like he has never even met me.

"I'm not going to jail like my father, Candy."

Levon peels out of the parking lot, leaving Jamal for dead. I know he probably would have killed me, but again I feel this surge of power and urgency, like I have to make my own decision now.

"Let me out, then."

"What?"

"Let me out."

"I kidnapped *you*, remember?"

"I'm not leaving him, Levon. I can't."

He looks at me hard, then turns his eyes back toward the road.

"Fuck!" he says and pulls a U-turn so hard that I hit my head on the side window.

"Ouch," I say, even though my tolerance for pain has risen considerably in the last twenty-four hours.

Back at the roadside bar, the parking lot is just as we left it. As we lift Jamal into the same trunk he threw me into, he moans slightly.

"I saw a hospital, back—"

"I know. I saw it too."

We drive there in silence, literally with blood on our sleeves. As we pull Jamal out of the trunk and place him under the neon lights of the ER entrance and jump back into the car, burning rubber, we actually start laughing. A second later though, we quiet down, realizing that it's not that funny.

We drive back to the motel in silence, both of us in shocked autopilot mode. There is nothing to say. What just went down is bigger in scope than either of us imagined. I could've been killed, and Jamal might even be dead by now.

We get back to our room, and I put the lamp back on the table, even though the lightbulb's been smashed in our scuffle. I try to clean up the shards, but my hands are shaking.

"Stop," Levon says. "Leave it."

He leads me into the bathroom and washes the blood from my arms. It's strangely intimate. He cleans himself after me, and then we grab what little stuff we have and we're off again.

Five miles down the highway, and I'm still shaking. We both keep looking back intermittently. Levon takes off his sweatshirt and says, "Put this on."

It's warm and smells like him, and it momentarily calms me.

"Do you think he'll die?"

"I don't know. I don't know," Levon repeats.

"It was self-defense, right?"

"Of course it was, Candy, of course." Levon is still trying to catch his breath.

"How did he find us?" I ask.

"There was a motorcycle. That he obviously stole. And he knew the route. There are only two motels in this town. I'm probably the only person the guy knows, and I have money. I was so stupid to trust him, but he was totally different when he was straight. Believable. And I couldn't do it alone. After he scored, everything went downhill. That's why I tried to pay him off."

"I knew when he was sitting on the cot, looking at me. He wasn't done."

"I thought he was. But we are going to have to drive a while, a different route, slightly west of here. We can't risk it…"

The car feels full of electricity, even with only the sound of the engine, the whir of the wheels.

"Did anyone see us? In the parking lot?" Levon asks.

"I don't think so."

"Candy, the game just changed."

It doesn't sound like his choice of words. But we are not our normal selves anymore. He keeps driving, my mind racing.

"I'm not leaving you alone again," he says softly but with conviction.

Say it again, I think. *Say it again.*

Chapter 13

The room we find is twenty miles west of I-95, and even though it feels way off the planned route Jamal knows about, I tell Levon to park down the block just in case.

The room has real wood paneling that smells like pine and a few framed pictures of rolling hills. I lock the double lock and sit against the door.

I keep thinking of the moment the trunk hit the bottom of Jamal's chin, his head flailing back, then the crunch when his head hit the rock. In the drug-like rush of power and adrenaline, those minutes felt completely transcendent.

Yes, I was acting in self-defense, but I never wanted anyone dead.

"Why did you want to leave him?" I ask Levon.

"Why did you insist on taking him?"

"I don't really know why. It was an instinct."

"I'm sorry."

"For what?"

"For not being there."

"Yeah, well, I'm used to that. My father's made a life of it."

"Well, you're not like your father at all."

"What's that supposed to mean?"

"Nothing. But there's something I have to tell you."

We each lie down on our separate beds, staring at the ceiling. I can hear crickets and the sound of firecrackers in the distance.

"What?" I ask.

"Jamal. He mentioned something he would do to you. Something I think is more horrible than even killing someone."

We both know what he's talking about. I put my hand up to my mouth to stop a scream.

"That's why," Levon says. "A person like that doesn't really need to be on this earth, right?"

"What if they change?"

Levon makes an agitated noise.

"Whatever. We did what you wanted."

"The right thing?"

"Who knows?"

"How did you actually find him?"

"There's a guy in my trailer park. Jamal was a friend of that guy's cousin. I didn't meet him until a day before we got you."

"Did he want part of the money?"

"He didn't know about the money, but he figured it out. I had planned on him just helping me at the beginning and paying him for his time. But then, in the parking lot, he tried to convince me to let him stay, to cut him in on the deal. I kept trying to give him more money to go away, but then he would score drugs and come back. And yeah, he knew the route. Following it was stupid of us."

We lay silent for a while. I can hear a mother scolding her kid as a car door slams. Normal people. I turn on the TV, then mute the sound. I need to know that else is happening, other dramas that are unfolding. Maybe even larger in scope than our own.

"What did your father not do? And how much do you want?"

Levon blinks slowly, and I can see his brain calculating.

"My grandmother," he says. "She's in this horrible home for old people. I want to get her out of there into a condo or something. She doesn't have much time left, and I don't want her to die there."

I knew there was more to him. Father wrongly accused, wants to help his grandmother. These are good attributes, right?

"But how does it all relate to Wade?"

"My dad worked for Wade, as a driver, in Miami."

When my father isn't on tour, he lives in a private villa on Shelter Island in Miami. I've only seen pictures of it in magazines and on the reality show.

"For how long?"

"Four years."

"If it wasn't drugs, then what was it?"

"Let's just say my dad took the fall for something Wade did."

"I can only imagine. The guy's a major slimeball."

"Like him?" Levon points to a Mexican drug-cartel leader on the TV screen.

"Yeah, if that guy wore skinny jeans and makeup."

Levon smiles, and it hits me what a strong person he must be. Willing to break the law for his father...

"How long have you been planning this?"

"Not long, actually. Wade promised my dad money. He's getting out soon, so he called Wade, who acted like he barely knew him."

"Typical," I say.

"Wade said something about tax evasion and the green river drying up or some shit, like he owed my dad fifty bucks. Hung up on him."

"How much did he promise your dad?"

"A million."

"What the… Is that what you're asking for? 'Cause you know, I'm fifty bucks, if that. He'd never give up a million for me."

"That's not what he's saying on TV."

"Well, he lies to the media all the time."

"We'll see."

"I guess so."

We watch the silent scene play out on the screen. When it goes to commercial, I turn to face him.

"Levon?"

"Yeah?"

"I don't want to go to jail."

He looks at me, nods, and then turns back to the TV. When the show comes back on, it's the end of the episode, and a woman is setting her house on fire. In a strange way, I can relate. Even though I know this trip has to have an end, it still feels like a beginning.

"He's not going to give you the money because of me. But you're right. Wade always does things for the sake of the public eye. It'll look bad if he doesn't pay my ransom. But how is it going to go down exactly?"

"I need to think about it some more," Levon says. "For now, let's just rest."

"OK."

But when he turns out the lights, my eyes stay wide open.

You don't think of these situations ever happening to you. But whatever happens, we are in it. There's no going back.

Chapter 14

The morning sun slices into the room, illuminating dust particles that hang and swirl in the stale air. As I wake up, I think about the Borings, Billy Ray, Fin, Rena, and Mrs. B. Are they all worried, or is it true that after forty-eight hours people start to forget?

I notice Levon also awake and staring into space from his own bed.

"So, what is it you're going to do?" I ask him. "After you help your grandmother, that is."

"Haven't thought that far."

"Who's the girlfriend?"

"Who?"

"The one in the picture you always look at."

"From Miami. A girl from Miami."

"And does this girl have a name?"

He sits up and stretches.

"What does she look like?"

"Red hair, short."

"Her hair is short, or she is short?"

"She is."

"That's it? You're supposed to say something like beautiful or ethereal."

"I don't even know what *ethereal* means."

"It means delicate or dreamlike. My mother was ethereal."

"Ah." He gets up and makes his way toward the bathroom.

"Do you think I'm ethereal?" I can't believe that question just came out of my mouth, but last night I may have accidentally killed someone, so I suppose anything is possible.

He smiles and says, "Sure."

"What about my hair? Do you like the blond?"

"It doesn't make you look dumb, if that's what you mean. I don't think you could ever look dumb."

He shuts the door to the bathroom.

When he gets out, I ask him a question I have been too freaked out to ask. "How did you find me and Jamal?"

"The hotel clerk told me which way the car went. I ran and then a lady picked me up. I spotted the car. That bar is the only place for miles."

I take a shower, breathing in his scent in the bathroom. It smells like a guy but in a good way.

Instead of breakfast, we load up on stuff from the vending machines.

"We're gonna have to go off the grid a little," he says, as we drive away from the freeway down a one-lane road.

There is uneasiness in my stomach, but watching Levon calms me. The way his strong hands hold the wheel, his bright eyes and half smile that are starting to feel like home.

For most of the day we just drive. We don't say it, but both of us know everything is different now. He is starting to open up to me, and we have been through a traumatic experience. Every once in a while we look at each other, acknowledging something happening, something bigger than ourselves.

There's a good chance Jamal is dead. And we might be wanted for murder.

As the afternoon light drains from the sky, the road we're on turns to dirt, and we come to a T with a line of mailboxes.

"Go right," I say, "and I can't tell you why."

Levon obeys, and we keep driving, the night slowly closing in on us.

"Do you still have the gun?" I ask.

He reaches under the seat and brings it out to show me, then puts it back.

"It's not loaded. It was my dad's."

"Levon, you have to tell me."

He sighs and scratches his head.

The car speeds into the descending darkness. There are no streetlights for miles in any direction.

"It was a big show in Miami. My dad never drove for Wade when he was performing, but he did that night. Normally, he drove a black town car, but that night Wade wanted a limo—a real tacky, white one. Everything was fine until we were on the way home. Wade told him to pull over. Your dad was, well, kind of trashed. He said he wanted to drive and that my dad should go in the back with Whisper."

"Whisper?"

"That was the girl's name. The dancer your dad picked up."

"I can only imagine what *her* deal was. OK, go on."

"So my dad's in the back, and Whisper's trying to give him a lap dance—and *boom*, the limo crashes into a storefront. They get out and there's glass everywhere, and Dad could hear sounds from under the car, animallike sounds."

My heart rate goes from soft rock to break beat. I turn to him.

"Was it an animal?"

"No, it was a homeless guy, and he was barely alive. Dad tried to call 911, but Wade stopped him. The guy was dying, but Wade wasn't having any of it. Sound familiar?"

"Wow."

Levon shakes his head, like he still can't wrap his mind around it. "My dad worked for him for four years. I knew Wade was crazy but not that crazy. Letting someone die?"

"Oh great, a charming man gets even charmier."

"You know that my reasons were different with Jamal, right?"

"Yes."

"So he finally let my dad call 911. But Wade made him say he was driving the car. Wade told him he'd only go to jail for a little while, that he'd give my dad a million when he got out. He also promised he'd look after my grandmother, which he's never done except to pay the bill for that horrible place she's in. Basically, he made it sound like a million dollars would solve everything. And my father just didn't want the guy to die."

"Did he?"

"Yes, a couple days later. He had other health problems, but the car accident..."

"Finished the job?"

"Basically. And my father was booked for vehicular manslaughter."

I am speechless. There's nothing else to say. I am so deeply ashamed that I can't speak. My father has sunken to a more subterranean low than I could've imagined. *Was that why he could never face me, because he knew what a dirtbag he was? Was that why I instinctually wanted to help Jamal? To be more like my mother than him?*

Our headlights cut through the thick night, illuminating the trees. I try to let the sound of the wheels and the hum of the engine lull me.

"Are you OK?" I ask Levon, who is wide awake.

"Yes, you can sleep. I'll drive."

Chapter
15

I wake up at dawn with a dry mouth. I find a Smartwater from days ago, and it tastes like heaven. We are parked in a turnout. Out the window I can see Levon peeing under a tree. For some reason, this makes me smile. If only life were that simple.

He gets back in the car and says, "Morning."

He folds open the vintage map, trying to figure out if we're still heading south.

"The sun is your best bet," I say groggily, pointing to where it's rising. "That's east, so south is that way." I point to our left.

He nods and starts to drive while eating crackers from our vending machine stash. The air comes through the car, and the sun slowly rises until it's shining directly at us. We both put our visors down at the same time, then turn to each other and smile.

"So what happened to Whisper?" I ask him.

"She took off. With my dad's favorite jacket around her shoulders."

He hands me a cracker. It's kind of stale, but I'm hungry so I don't care.

"And you know all this from..."

"Visiting my dad in jail every Wednesday for two years."

"Does he know you're doing this? That you came to get me?"

"No."

For the next few minutes, new thoughts race around in my brain, trying to catch up with one another. I may be having an epiphany. As I eat the rest of the crackers, I devise a plan, wondering if I'm crazy or if it could really work.

We get to a point where to keep going south, we have to get back on I-95, which cuts through the trees in an arc over Lake Marion, near Charleston. There's barely anyone on the highway, but we both check the mirrors every time a car approaches.

"So what's up with the green backpack? You said it was a gift."

"Yeah, from this kid I know, Kyle." His half smile returns when he says the kid's name.

"That look… It was on your face when you first saw me."

"It was?"

"Yes."

"Well, you weren't what I expected."

"How do you mean?"

"Not sure. You just seemed different."

"OK, I'll take it. I never want to be what's expected."

Now his smile has returned, full blown.

"So, tell me about Kyle."

"Well, he's a kid from my trailer park. I hang out with him. He's got no one, basically. His parents are major deadbeats."

I watch his eyes go soft, which I've never seen before. Almost misty.

"I used to take him out on my friend's refurbished Jet Ski, and we'd get hot dogs from the food carts near South Beach. We're tight." He pauses, and since I can only see his profile, I can't tell if he's choking up or clearing his throat.

"So, he gave you the backpack?"

"Yes."

"Cool."

"He made the money from his lemonade stand, and he knows my favorite color is green, so…"

Now I'm the one who's getting choked up.

"Sounds like an awesome kid."

"Yeah. Anyway, he loves music, so one of the things I want to get him is an iPod with those red headphones, you know?"

"Beats by Dr. Dre. Overrated, but great for kids."

"Yeah, those. Anyway, I know the backpack is, like, cheesy or whatever, but I love it."

I look in the backseat, and there it is, next to my Hello Kitty bag. Electric green and super shiny.

"I could tell. You did *not* want me making fun of it."

He chuckles a little, changing his grip on the wheel.

A motorcycle passes us on the left, and we both tense up. Jamal is the conversation we don't need to have. We are both still wondering if he's even alive.

I grab the map. Jacksonville is the next colored-in circle.

"We need to avoid Jacksonville like the plague," I say. "Just in case."

We pass a couple of RVs and an old Ford driven by a guy with a gray ponytail and a smirk on his face.

Does he know who we are?

Eventually we pull over for gas, and on my way back

117

from the bathroom, I ask a lady where the nearest library is. Levon finishes pumping, runs inside, and comes back with a bottle of Gatorade and a stuffed alligator. I put it next to the turtle on the dash.

"We should give them names," I say.

"How about Mortimer and Randolph?" he offers.

"Ha! How do you know *Trading Places?*"

"It was one of the six movies we owned."

"But you've watched a lot, right?"

"My whole life."

"I knew it, 'cause you knew *The Godfather*. Do you know the film game?" I ask.

"No."

"OK, if I name a film you have to name an actor in it. If I name an actor you have to name a film they were in, et cetera. If two actors are named consecutively, you have to say a film they were in together."

"OK."

"I'll start easy," I tell him. "*When Harry Met Sally.*"

"Meg Ryan."

"Tom Hanks."

"*Sleepless in Seattle*," he says like it's obvious.

"Ha. Bet that was one part of your collection. OK, this is where it gets harder, because I now have to name someone else that was in *Sleepless in Seattle*. Hmm. Oh! Victor Garber."

"Wow. Do TV shows count?"

"Nope."

"OK, hang on...*Argo*."

"Brilliant film! Well, my friend, this is where I trump you. Alan Arkin."

He thinks for a second, then bangs the steering wheel in a burst of defeat. Another motorcycle passes on the other side of the highway, and my mind flashes to Jamal and his blood running into the dirt—first red, then turning black. I touch my head where I banged it on the jack. It's still tender.

"Where'd you get the money to do all this anyway?"

"Saved up. I cut grass."

I picture him shirtless in the Florida sun, the roar of the mower and the sweat running from his chest down the ridges of his torso.

"And let me guess, you're going to split the ransom money, if there is any, with your dad?"

He nods. "I want to get the money before he gets out."

"Well, I have a proposition for you."

He rolls his eyes like he's used to it but still ready to hear me out.

"I want retribution too. So let's work together."

"How?"

"You and I both know it's not about money, Levon. I mean you'll get the money, I hope. But your father went to jail, and it should have been mine."

"So…"

"Whisper is our key. If we can find her and she'll testify, we can put my father away. Trust me, if it involves a rock star, cops will want to reopen the case."

"What are you, a detective now?"

"All they have is your father's testimony, right?"

"Yeah."

"So, you said the accident happened in downtown Miami. Like, near businesses and stuff?"

"Right in the heart of it."

"Then there'll be surveillance tapes. They even have them in streetlights now. If they go back to find it, they'll see that Wade was driving."

"That's a long shot."

"Not at all. Especially if we have Whisper. Let's start with the club. Do you know it? Where she danced?"

"I knew the one my dad went to, so that's probably the same one."

He speeds up a little, and I can tell I've got his juices

flowing, even though he always plays it cool. I'm becoming better at reading him.

I reach over and grip the forearm I've been staring at for days. "And, Levon, listen to me. Whatever happens, you're not going to jail. I'll say it was consensual. I know people saw you forcefully take me, but I'll say I knew you, that it was our plan all along."

Levon focuses hard on the road. We pass a semi, its roar invading our ears. Then it's just the whir of the wind.

"Wade should be punished for not keeping his word. Not to mention being a lame father, but killing someone and sending your dad to jail? He needs to go down."

I see a trace of a nod. *How can someone be so sexy when he's just thinking?*

"Let's stop at the library in Charleston. They'll have Internet."

He looks skeptical.

"We'll be in and out."

"OK."

We exit off of the highway and immediately see a sign for the library. When we get there, we enter the parking lot slowly, making sure there are no cops. We park, get out, and walk through the library's grand entrance and onto the cool black-and-white tile. There are six computers against a wall.

The two on each end are unoccupied. It's mostly kids playing online games, but there's one guy who looks like a journalist type, so I choose the one farthest from him. Yes, I've watched too many movies, but that's coming in handy. I'm liking our whole adventure again, even though I'm still a little nauseous thinking that we may be wanted for murder.

"What was the name of the club?" I ask Levon. "The one your dad went to."

He has to think for a moment. "Kit Kat!" He practically jumps from the chair he pulled up. Then he scans the room to see if anyone is noticing us.

"Calm down," I tell him, but I'm thrilled. It feels like we're really a team now.

I google the club, which is now called the King of Diamonds. Then I google both with the name "Whisper," but nothing comes up. Still, I write down the address. While Levon goes to the bathroom, I log on to my Gmail again, and there's another note from Billy Ray.

From: tapwaterrocks@yahoo.com
To: candyfromastranger@gmail.com
Subject: senior moment

Candy Cane—

I saw you on the news again. I hope you're OK. I wanted to let you know, I ran into your grandmother in the Safeway, and she was talking to the melons. She didn't recognize me, so I was worried. The cops had to take her home. I think she's losing it. I miss you.

Billy Ray

Not now, I think. *Not while I'm gone. Figures that's the only time she needs me.*

I quickly set up another email account so it's not traceable and write Billy Ray back.

From: gonegirlthankgod@hotmail.com
To: tapwaterrocks@yahoo.com
Subject: omg

Billy—

I'm OK. I've been kidnapped, and some crazy shit has happened, but I'm actually having a good time. Thank you for letting

me know about Rena. I will call her soon,
but in the meantime, could you please
check on her? Also, send me an MP3 of
your solo stuff.

C

Just as I hit Send, I sense someone approaching. I can
hear high-heeled shoes click on the tiles, getting louder with
each step. I quit out of the screen and turn to see what looks
like the head librarian in a sensible suit, hair in a tight bun,
thin-rimmed glasses. She is holding a newspaper with my
junior picture plastered on the cover, alongside the same
picture they always use of my dad, scarves dangling like
snakes from his microphone stand, his mouth in mid-wail.

"Excuse me…" she says, like she might have just discov-
ered something important.

Before I get a chance to say anything, Levon starts
motioning behind her back for us to get out of there. He
points toward the back door, then leaves out the front. I
look down and pass by her quickly, simply saying, "Sorry…"

I scoot behind the stacks of books and glance back. Two
policemen are entering the library. The librarian approaches
them, then points in my direction.

Shit.

I have to think of a diversion fast. I look to my left, where there's an emergency door. I grab a hardback copy of *Gone with the Wind* and hurl it toward the door, and it's a bull's-eye. The alarm goes off. I crouch and start crawling toward the back exit. As the policeman and the librarian run toward the emergency door, I jump down the length of steps and sneak out the back. When I get outside, Levon is waiting in the car. I jump in, and we literally burn rubber. We both holler as we pass the empty, parked cop car, speeding away.

He heads toward the highway.

"No, we need to hide. Take this dirt road up here."

He obeys, and we speed down it, kicking up dust in our wake. It's dusk, the last bit of light lingering. The road goes on for a few miles, until we come to some train tracks. We pull up to the tracks, he shuts off the ignition, and we turn to each other, laughing in spite of it all.

"She was just a librarian!" I say.

"She knew though. She knew who you were. She was holding the newspaper."

"That could have been a coincidence—seriously."

"I don't think so. Why were the cops there?"

"Maybe Jamal is alive and talked? Anyway, we should stay on back roads."

"You think?"

I give him a look. It's weird to hear him say something *I* normally would. As we lock eyes, smiling, the blinking lights on the train crossing flash red, and the signal starts to repeatedly *ding* like the ticking of a loud clock.

To our right, a train whistles as it approaches, smoke billowing above it in a thick cloud.

Then we hear another sound that literally makes our heads hit the ceiling. Sirens. Two squad cars, coming at us from behind. They pull to a stop, and we hear a loud voice over the intercom speaker.

"Please get out of the vehicle with your hands above your head. I repeat…"

The train is getting closer.

"Please get out of the vehicle."

I feel my heart clench, twisting up into my throat.

This is it. This is the end of our fun.

Levon stares straight ahead. Slowly, he puts the car in Drive, inching up so the car is directly over the train tracks. My instinct is to get out, to run, but I can't move. I just look to my right at the train rapidly approaching and yell, "*Go!*"

We peel out across the tracks and the train speeds by, nabbing the rear bumper and causing our car to fishtail. I look back at the train, the cops now stuck behind it. Then I look at Levon, who is yelling at the top of his lungs. I start to yell too, and we are full of adrenaline, speeding off into who knows where, not even looking back.

Chapter 16

O h my God," I keep saying over and over. "Oh my God. Oh my God."

Levon takes a left down another dirt road, then a right, like he knows where he's going. He is driving fast—really fast—but for some crazy reason I'm not afraid. *What could be worse than what just happened? Or more exhilarating?*

It's completely dark now, and there's a thin layer of dust in our car.

"Levon...what the..."

"I saw it in a movie once," he says, still breathing hard.

I look at him.

"So, you thought you'd just try it out?"

"I waited a little too long."

"A second longer and we'd be street meat."

This makes him laugh, but I'm not sure if it's just nerves.

"You do realize the chances of us making it to Miami are now slim to none?"

"Not if we ditch the car and change our look again," he says.

"OK, well, that's a good plan. But what are we going to do tonight—sleep in a bush?"

"I don't know. We need to drive some more."

I let the wind brush my face, thinking about Rena in the grocery store losing it. It's hard to picture because she's always so stern and held together. I know I have to call her, but right now I just want to be free of everything.

"I didn't think you had that in you," I say. "What you did back there."

"I didn't either. I just didn't want it to…"

"End?"

Before he has a chance to answer, we come to an actual end—of the road—which is a driveway to an old farm. There are two barns and a small house with the front porch light on. The paint is peeling, and there are mud boots lined up near the door. A farmer guy, probably in his sixties, walks out, waving us over.

"Act innocent," Levon says. "We're lost is all. OK?"

"Got it."

The farmer peers into the car on my side, and I can smell beer on his breath. His white beard is crusty in a few places, and his teeth are crooked, but his smile is kind.

"You two must have lost your way."

Levon is quiet again, and I know this is where my skills have to compensate.

"Yeah, we're doing research for a school project. We decided to go off the beaten path a little."

"That's me. Off the beaten path!"

A silence descends, and he stares at us.

"Just kidding. I'm Jerry."

"Nice to meet you. You know it's getting late and…"

"What happen to your bumper, son?"

Levon shrugs it off. "Someone rear-ended me while I was parked," he says rather unconvincingly.

"Jerry, do you think we could stay here for the night?" I ask.

Jerry acts like he's mulling it over, but I can tell he's tickled. Probably not used to visitors.

"It just so happens you young'uns are in luck. I've got an old silo the day laborers sleep in sometimes. It's got two bunks. It's no great shakes, but you're welcome to it for the night."

"Do you think I could park behind it?" Levon asks.

"No, you can park right here."

"OK," I say, figuring we'll deal with that issue later.

The silo is this huge, round structure that once held wheat or grain or something. As Jerry promised, there are two wrought-iron bunks and a large wooden box that's turned over to make a table. Jerry lights the two candles that are on the box and gives us blankets that were stashed underneath it. When he leaves, I say, "You know, he totally could come out here in the middle of the night and, like, slaughter us."

Levon chuckles.

"Jerry's all right. I think he likes you though."

"Tell him to take a number," I say.

Levon grimaces.

"Ever been in a silo before?"

"No. Ever been stuffed in a trunk?"

"Yes. And it's worse than it seems in the movies. I passed out from the fumes."

"Well, that whole thing started with stupid me going to get this after my run."

He pulls a pint of whiskey out of his green bag, unscrews it, takes a huge gulp, and passes it to me. I do the same. It slides down my throat, heating my blood and blurring the edges of my sharp thoughts.

We are in a silo in candlelight. The cops could come at any minute, but I feel like I'm exactly where I'm supposed to be.

We pass the bottle back and forth.

"OK, let's play the film game again but add directors to the mix. I'll start with a director, then you have to either name an actor or a film he or she directed. If you name a film, I have to name another actor in the film. If you name an actor, I have to name either another actor in the same film or another director that directed that actor. Get it?"

"Uh...I think so."

"OK, we'll start easy again. Woody Allen."

"*Annie Hall*," he says.

"OK, *Blue Jasmine*."

"Haven't seen that," he says sheepishly.

"Cate Blanchett, I think she won an Oscar. My favorite of hers, though, was *Babel*."

He turns, the light behind his green eyes burning into me.

"Wait a second, you know *Babel*?"

"It's one of my top five," I say, and it feels like I'm revealing some deep, dark secret.

"Me too. I saw it when it came out, although I was way too young. I snuck into the theater. I thought about it a lot."

We smile at each other like we can't really control what our faces are doing. We drink and play the movie game some more, until we hear the creak of the huge sliding door of the silo. It's Jerry, and he's carrying an old-fashioned lantern.

"OK, you two. I'm not harboring fugitives. I just watched the news. Do you know they're calling you Bonnie and Clyde? You've got five minutes to get out of here, or I'm calling the sheriff."

We scramble to get our stuff, and on the way out Levon stumbles, the whiskey falling out of his bag.

Jerry grabs the bottle, walks over to Levon, and holds it out to him.

"You and me, we never met. This never happened, you got it?"

"Got it," Levon says, taking the whiskey. We get back in the car and pull away. There are a million stars, which are brighter than the weak headlights of our Toyota.

"Bonnie and Clyde," I say.

"I guess we should rob some banks now," Levon adds.

"Yeah, but they died in the end."

He doesn't answer. I can't really tell, but it looks like he's nodding off. I'm not in much better shape, but still, I offer to drive.

"It's fine, Candy. I'm fine. I'm just going to go over here…for a while." He turns onto a road that's more like a path, towering corn on either side. He drives and drives until we can't drive anymore, then we get out. I grab Mortimer and Randolph and shove them into my bag. I'm not superstitious, but they haven't let us down so far. We stumble farther and farther into the stalks of corn until our exhaustion kicks in and we collapse.

Chapter 17

I wake up in Levon's arms, an army of corn stalks standing proud around us.

I have no idea how this happened, and even though we could get caught at any moment, I feel safer than I've ever felt.

I don't move for what seems like an hour. I breathe with him as his chest rises and falls. We are in the middle of a cornfield at the crack of dawn. A curious bird on one of the stalks is staring at us like we don't belong here.

When he wakes, Levon is confused and kind of scoots

away from me. I don't register the slight, just propel into business mode.

"We've gotta go on foot. We can't go back for the car."

Levon still has a Smartwater in his bag. He hands it to me first, and after I swill it, I hand it back to him. He dumps it over his face.

We walk through the cornfields for what feels like hours, until we come to a clearing. There's a bus stop that is obviously not a bus stop anymore and an abandoned cruiser bicycle.

Levon takes me behind a tree and pulls his shaver out of his bag, along with a clip for hair.

"You want me to shave my head?"

He nods.

"Well, I've attacked a meth head, been stuffed in a trunk, played suicide with a train, and slept in a cornfield, so I'm thinking shaving my head is a no-brainer."

I turn my back to him as he clicks on the razor. The hair falls in clumps at my feet, and my head feels like it's floating. I touch it, then turn around to look at Levon, who's smiling wide.

"You have a nicely shaped head," he says.

"I would have preferred something like *You look great*, but..."

"No! You do!"

"Whatever. What about you?"

He pulls the cowboy hat I picked out at Walmart out of his bag and puts it on.

"It does make you look different," I say.

"In a good way?"

"Let's just say *different*."

He smiles and walks over to the bike, checking the tires.

"The rear one's pretty flat, but it might get us somewhere."

I sit on the front handlebar as Levon pedals. It takes us a while to get going. We are laughing like this is any other day, like we are not fugitives breaking the law.

We ride the shoulder of a paved road, and it looks like there's a town ahead. The bike's tire becomes completely flat so we ditch it and walk the rest of the way. We come to an old-school diner. Levon tells me to wait outside, then goes inside. A few minutes later, he comes out with two cinnamon rolls, handing one to me. As we walk toward a used-car lot, I eat mine, not remembering when food ever tasted this good. I moan a little, and Levon smiles. "Awesome, huh?"

"Sugar, cinnamon, and buttery bread… Can't go wrong."

"Stay here," he says when we get to the lot.

It's pretty much a miracle that twenty minutes later, Levon drives off the lot in a rusty pickup truck.

"Get in," he says.

I do, and the inside is just as battered as the outside—ripped seats, sun-faded dash, a gaping hole where the stereo used to be.

"How much was this?"

"Twelve hundred, with temporary plates and insurance. Which means I've basically got nothing left."

I look at the gas gauge.

"Well, at least the tank is full."

He looks at me incredulously, my secret cowboy.

Minutes later, we are back on the highway. The truck makes a high-pitched whine when it goes over sixty, but after a while I get used to it.

I lean toward Levon so he can hear me over the noise.

"We should just go to the club when we get to Miami and ask about Whisper, start there."

He doesn't say anything.

"What was your original plan?" I ask.

"There's a Black Angels show on Friday," he says. "At that theater."

"What day is it today?"

"Tuesday."

"So, you were just going to show up at his dressing room?"

"Actually, I wasn't sure. I hadn't thought that far ahead.

138

By now, he knows I have you. So the more time that goes by, the more desperate he'll be."

"He doesn't care, Levon. Trust me."

"But you said, since it's in the press…"

"We have to find Whisper and reopen the case. Do you know who the detective is, the one who put your dad away?"

"Yes. And he's still at the Miami PD."

"Perfect. We'll call him after we find Whisper."

He looks at me like I'm some kid playing a made-up game.

"This is real, Levon. We can do this. We need to do this."

He doesn't say anything, just shakes his head again, except now with that half smile teasing his lips.

As we start to see signs for Savannah, the air gets thicker and the songs on the radio get twangier. We pull into a Red Roof Inn. The door is red, but the roof is brown.

In the parking lot, Levon tells me to stay in the car. I explain about Billy's email and tell him I'm going to call Rena. He thinks about it.

"Don't worry. I'll hang up before they can trace it again."

"OK."

As he walks toward the lobby, I film him again on my handheld, even though I'm not supposed to. His butt is high in his jeans, and his arms sway ever so slightly. After he goes inside, I turn the camera toward me and smile.

I dial Rena, and she answers on the fourth ring.

"It's me. Are you OK?"

"Yes. Candy, where are you?"

"I'm in North Carolina," I lie. "Like I said, I'm safe. It will all be over soon. But Billy told me you had to be taken home by the police."

"Just confused. I'm fine. Wade called, looking for you."

"Tell him he's a little late to the party."

"What?"

"Never mind. Rena, hang in there, OK? I'll try to come home after all this is over. Before I have to go back to school."

"Tomorrow?"

"No, maybe Sunday. I have to go. I love you."

"I love you," she says back, and I have to stare at the phone to make sure I heard it correctly. I hang up as tears gather and pool in my eyes, threatening to overflow. No one except my mother has ever said those words to me. I'm not one to feel sorry for myself, but I notice Mortimer and Randolph—who I replaced on the pickup's dash—looking at me with such innocence that I have to wonder where mine has gone.

By the time Levon comes back, I'm convulsing in sobs.

"Hey," he says tenderly, and I try to pull myself together.

"What is it?"

140

"My grandmother told me she loved me."

"Well, isn't that a good thing?"

"I guess so," I say, and we both laugh a little.

He opens my door and helps me out, holds my hand all the way to our room, which is clean and smells like Pine-Sol. The TV is a flat screen, and the beds have pillow-top mattresses. I plop onto mine and say, "Moving up in the world."

Levon jumps onto his own bed and says, "Better than a cornfield."

"I thought you said you were out of money."

"I am, but I still have the card. I'm surprised it still works."

"This place is like Shangri-la."

"Where the hell is Shangri-la anyway?"

"I don't know."

We both start laughing again, then he turns on the TV. We watch the news for a while, but nothing comes up about Bonnie and Clyde. The report probably already aired at the top of the hour.

"Candy, I forgot to tell you... Nice job with the fire alarm," he says.

"Nice job on the train tracks."

He walks over to my bed, sits down next to me, and cups his hand on my cheek for a second. His smile drops from his face, and I'm pulled into his magnetic gaze, his bottle-green eyes staring at me with what I could only describe as truth.

Then he kisses me, long and slow, and there is only this moment.

Chapter

18

This morning we have a pseudo-waitress for breakfast. She is very wholesome looking, but there is a message written up her arm, the words consonant heavy—I'm guessing in some northern European language. She assumes I'm Levon's girlfriend, and I try to play down the smile that is forcing its way onto my face. After the kiss, and I will call it *the* kiss for its epic, mind-expanding qualities, he turned the light out and we went to sleep. But we were both awake in the dark for a while. It took all the strength I had not to get up and into his bed.

"So, what was the worst thing you did?" I ask him as I try to squish the rock-hard butter onto my frail toast. "I mean, besides sneak into the movies."

"Taking you."

"Besides that."

He sips his coffee, pondering the question.

"Well, when I was in high school, I used to read to this blind woman. She was pretty funny. She'd ask me to read weird things like obituaries and statistics for random sports like rowing. Once I even read her names out of the phone book."

"Ha."

"She liked the names that started with *P* for some reason. I think she just wanted to hear someone talk. Anyway, she paid me twenty-five dollars a session, and one day, she gave me two twenties instead of a twenty and a five—and I didn't tell her."

I look at him, waiting for him to smile or laugh, but his face is even.

"You're not serious."

The thing is, he *is* serious. I almost spit out my toast.

"That's pretty bad," I say, trying to keep a straight face, but it's not working.

"Shut up."

"No, it's sweet," I say. But because of my usual sarcasm, he's not convinced.

Levon takes a bite of his scrambled eggs, dabbing at the corner of his mouth with his napkin.

"I went back three years later," he says softly.

"What?"

"I paid her back three years later. I was still thinking about it."

"And…"

"She told me I was crazy, but she thanked me. And then she gave me the money back. She said it was the gesture that mattered, that I should keep the money. I still have it. I'm not going to spend it."

He is completely serious, and my heart flutters. Then his face blanches as he sees something behind me on the TV. I turn around. They are running a sketch of Levon, a crude pencil drawing that makes him look mean. Did they get that from the librarian? The hospital? In the drawing, the eyes are dead, which is so not him. Even when he's melancholy or lost in thought, his eyes have a shimmer to them.

The picture of me is different, with hair past my shoulders. Did they get that from Rena? I touch my head to confirm my hair is gone. My scalp feels bristly in a good way. I looked in the mirror this morning, but only for an instant, afraid of what I might see. More than my look. I've been kissed before, but never like by Levon.

There's a kid with a sailor hat, eating with his apathetic parents and watching the TV while he nibbles on one of the stale muffins. There is a picture of the Toyota, which they obviously found, and another sketch of Jamal, who they mention was "admitted to the hospital with critical head injuries." The sketch could be any black man; it doesn't look like Jamal at all. Then again, he didn't look like himself with his head split open. Leaving him in that parking lot would have been a Wade Rex move, and even though I appreciate that Levon wanted to protect me, I feel like we did the right thing.

"Finish up," Levon says. "We have to make it to North Miami tonight. You can sleep in the back. You were tossing and turning last night."

"You were too."

We stare at each other, both of us turning red. For an instant, I feel like he's going to kiss me again.

"C'mon," he says.

As we walk by the family, the kid with the sailor hat points at us and says, "You were on TV!" His parents look up, then at the TV, which is playing a weather segment.

"Johnny, don't be silly," the mother says.

"I saw him!" the boy says, putting on a grim face.

The waitress, who has overheard everything, walks over. "Wait a second… Was that you?"

"There must be a misunderstanding. I'm not an actor," Levon says.

He's learning.

"No! It was on the news!" the boy says.

"Shh," the mother says.

"It wasn't me. I'm Jack. Jack Hacken."

I grab his arm and say, "Let's go, Jack. We're late."

The waitress's eyes narrow, but we don't stop.

We go back to the hotel room and get our stuff together in seconds.

"Jack Hacken?" I ask, throwing my bag over my shoulder.

"It wasn't my best moment."

"Well, let's get out of here."

As we leave, I turn at the threshold of the door and say, "Bye, nice hotel room."

"Rooms don't have ears," Levon says.

"Think of all the secrets they'd have if they did," I say.

As we head down the stairs toward the car, a skinny man smoking in his doorway gives me a greasy smile, and I flip him the bird.

Back on the highway, I start to feel that adrenaline again.

Like it all could end at any minute. Especially if that wait-ress calls the cops like the librarian did. I decide to make the most of the situation. See if I can dig deeper into Levon.

"What's your father like?"

"He's cool. He always had my back."

"Did you ever try to contact your mother?"

"It didn't matter, Candy. He was all I needed. I know they say kids need both parents, but do they, really? Look how you turned out."

I roll the window down to get more air. I hope he's not looking at me, because my face is probably caving into itself.

"I had my mother…for seven years at least."

"Yeah."

"So, you never answered my question. After your grand-mother's set up, what do you want to do?"

"Really?"

"Yes."

"Buy an art-house movie theater, with a café maybe. Run it. Show whatever films I want."

"That sounds like a great plan." I roll down the window even more. The landscape looks polished, brighter. The trees are green; the sun is high. I've been kissed by an outlaw. I can almost feel his full lips, covered with a dull sheen of sweet whiskey. When we finished, we both took intakes of breath, neither of us wanting to let them out. We were suspended in time.

I stick my hand out the window, curling it like a wave through the air.

"You know, when I'm eighteen, I'll get a ton of cash. I could invest in your theater, if you let me screen my own movie."

"What movie?"

"A gritty kidnapping story."

He glances at me, and I swear his eyes smolder for a second.

"Kidding!"

"You better be."

He checks the rearview. A black car approaches us from behind. It looks like it could be an unmarked police car.

"Don't worry. We aren't linked to the truck," I tell him.

"Unless the waitress…"

"I don't think…"

He steps on the gas a little.

"No speeding," I say.

"Got it," he says, slowing down.

He looks over at me with his almost smile.

"What?"

"That haircut makes you look powerful."

"Is that a good thing or a bad thing?"

The black car passes us, and the coast is clear for now.

"It's a good thing. So, what made you get into movies?" Levon asks.

"They've always been my escape. One good thing about my grandmother is she has no idea about parental controls, or even the difference between ratings. I watched *Nightmare on Elm Street* when I was eight and *Primal Fear* when I was twelve. I've seen every movie by Quentin Tarantino, Spike Lee, Woody Allen, and my favorite director, John Hughes. Eventually I started making my own. It's the only time I feel truly myself."

"And being kidnapped?"

"That too."

"So what are you working on now?"

"Well, since I've been at NRS, I've made two short films no one has seen except Fin the janitor."

"Who's that?"

"A friend. He once dressed up and pretended to be my dad for a school event. It was funny. His suit was too big."

"So, you're friends with the janitor?"

"Yeah, you got a problem with that?"

"No, it's cool. As long as he's not trying to…"

"It's not like that."

Not like you, I don't say.

"Anyway, there's only one filmmaking elective, and you have to be a senior to take it. When I do, I'm gonna make a film about a homeless guy."

"Hmm."

"There's this town called Northampton near my school. It's, like, Freakville. There's this one guy. His name is Gary. He hosts a poetry reading every week on the street. He's got a crazy, super-layered past. I want to do an exposé, a gritty doc, and call it *There's Something about Gary*."

Levon smiles, getting the reference.

"So, where will your art-house cinema be?"

"I'm thinking Albuquerque, New Mexico," he says.

"Hmm. Why Albuquerque?"

"There's one for sale there, so I've been researching it. New Mexico is cool. It's sunny a lot, and it's a big-sky kind of place. Opening the theater might be a dumb move, but in the right city it could work, and I think Albuquerque's it."

"I can picture it. I can see it happening."

He gives me a dubious look until he realizes I'm serious. All of a sudden I want to make it my life mission to go to Albuquerque. I imagine him inside his trailer, counting the days until freedom, dreaming of open spaces and flick-ering projectors.

We pass a sign that says "Welcome to Georgia, State of Adventure."

We both read it, then look at each other and smile. He takes one hand off the steering wheel and cups it under mine. I try to act like it's a totally normal gesture, but my heart starts to pound. Not from being caught or chased or thrown in a trunk.

Because I've wanted him to do that for days.

Chapter 19

S omething is different.

School seems like a dot in the distance, which it is.

An outlaw is holding my hand, and the wind is tick-
ling my scalp. We continue to drive until I can't take the
silence anymore.

"So, why didn't your dad try to appeal his charges?"

"He's waiting for the money. That million would change
his life."

"That's a long time to pay for someone else's crime."

"He should never have let Wade drive. But he was afraid
of him."

"He *is* kind of a bully. Have you met him?"

"Yeah. He's funny, but what a major ego! He paid my dad well though and always had his back—to a fault."

"A San Andreas fault."

He barks out another laugh. "True."

We stop at a rest stop and each go to our separate bathrooms. In mine, I finally look at myself full on. My eyes seem doubled and my cheeks more narrowed. My lips are bigger. The entire proportions of my face have changed, but I like it. Next to me I see a woman putting on makeup and feel a pang of sadness, knowing that it's never going to help the ruin of her face. Next to her, a young girl in an oversize sweatshirt washes her round, pale face that seemingly has no pores. I think of myself as a kid, just like her, living through a maze of bathrooms, rest stops, green rooms, and hotel restaurants. Maybe that's why this feels so right. I was raised on the road, and I needed to get back here, see real reminders of humanity, and plug into the raw, constantly moving world.

When I return to the car, it's locked, and Levon's not back yet. I sit on the hood, and a middle-aged woman approaches me with concern. I'm ready to deny knowing anything about Candy Rex or a kidnapping, but she simply asks how I'm doing.

154

"Fine."

"You on a family trip?"

"You could call it that," I say with a smile.

"We are too, but it seems like we can't get anywhere with all these stops!"

I don't know what to say. She stands there awkwardly, and I wonder if she's bluffing and knows my face from TV, even with my shaved head. The kid at breakfast did. I look around the rest stop for any leering presences. Just the usual dirty truckers and potbellied fathers. The woman gives me a warm smile and heads to the bathroom as Levon walks out. I imagine we are together on a family trip, off to see the in-laws or to some posh resort. We could have fun together. We already are.

In the car, he asks, "Who was that?"

"Just a weird housewife from some RV."

"Was she onto you?"

"A little, but nothing to worry about."

The road stretches on, and though we glance in the rearview from time to time, it's mostly blurred trees and Mortimer and Randolph looking at us from the dash. The sun beats down from the highest point in the sky.

I lean my head against Levon's shoulder. After a while, my neck starts to hurt, so he lifts his arm and puts it

around me. I wish once again that the road would just
go on and on. This feels like the closest thing to home
I've got.

"So why do you hate boarding school so much? The
grounds looked amazing."

"Don't get me wrong. It's a beautiful place, and some
of my teachers are really cool, and I get that I'm privileged
to go there, but the other students... I'm not aligned with
them socially, if that makes sense. You know, I didn't mind
growing up with a rock band. I just wish my mother hadn't
died on me. And part of me blames my father."

"Why?"

"I don't know. He's easy to blame, I guess."

"You know I'm not a huge fan of Wade, obviously, but
maybe he had nothing to do with it."

I sit up and look at him.

"I doubt it. Do you know I had a dream where I was
just punching him in the stomach over and over? It was
super uplifting."

He smiles. "Candy, I'm not trying to stand up for him,
believe me, but as I said before, you turned out fine."

I try to give him a sultry look and say, "Dating material?"

"Yeah," he says, but I'm not sure if he means for him.
Does he really like the other girl, the one in the picture?

Now that we've kissed, it's like we're in the foyer of a house. Will the door open to other rooms? Does he think I'm loyal to Billy Ray? Yes, I went to third base with him and the kid worships me, but he's not boyfriend material. Sexy offspring of wrongly accused convicts are more my style, and yes, I watch too many movies.

Eventually, I ask the question we've been avoiding. I have to.

"So, do you think he's dead?"

"I don't know, Candy. You have to remember that whatever you did was unintentional. You were trying to protect yourself."

He's right, but still, I can't stop seeing Jamal's head, snapping back, and the terrible sound of his head hitting the rock.

"Will they charge us for murder?"

"They could, but I don't think…"

He looks in the side mirror, then back at me.

"I don't think he will be missed, if you know what I mean. I don't think he had any family."

"Are you sure?"

"Not positive, but pretty sure. He was vague about it."

I wonder who would miss me if I died. Rena. Billy Ray. Fin. That's about it. But maybe I can add another person to that list. The person in the cowboy hat, driving this car, steering us to some great unknown.

I fall asleep with my head against the window, and when I wake up, the sun is setting, making the sky scream out in every shade of red, orange, and pink. Wisps of clouds behind the trees change hue even as I look at them. It reminds me how fast the world goes. Our lives, our experiences—so impermanent. I loved my mother more than anything in the world, and maybe that was because I knew she would be taken away from me. Our connection was even stronger because we had no longevity. We were fated to self-destruct. Is it the same with me and Levon?

I stick my camera out the window to catch the red sky before it fades to black.

Chapter
20

It sounds like a gun going off right next to my head and scares the living crap out of me.

"Shit." Levon swerves into the breakdown lane. We've lost the right front tire.

He tells me to stay put and gets out, starts searching around the back, and then he slams the trunk closed and gets back into the driver's seat.

"There's a spare but no jack," he says. "Grab your stuff. We're gonna have to hitch."

We stand in back of the truck, holding out our thumbs, the cars shooting past us at astronomical speeds. After a while, an eighteen-wheeler honks and slows down. Without saying anything, we run to catch up to it.

The trucker opens the door, and we climb up and in. His hair is greasy, and his two front teeth are capped in gold. He reeks of body odor.

"Got a flat?" he asks.

"Yeah," Levon says. "Could you take us to the next town?"

"Sure, glad to help," he says.

He starts up the truck, and we pull back into the lane. His hair is combed over, and his stomach protrudes out to the wheel. He looks like he hasn't showered in weeks.

The radio is playing Christian rock. Something about *He is the one who will save us.* I grab Levon's hand and squeeze it. No one says anything for a while, and we pass a couple exits where there were obviously towns.

"The next exit will be fine," I tell him.

"Well, beggars can't be choosers," the trucker says, laughing a little to himself.

I look at Levon, who's trying to stay cool, his other hand inside his bag. *Is he gripping the gun?*

The radio sings about Judgment Day. I try not to look at the trucker.

Finally, he pulls over into a rest area, parks, and says,

"You two just stay put. Back in a flash." He gets out, then clicks the automatic lock.

We try to open the doors manually but they don't. *Is this guy psycho?* We look for a button to let us out.

"It has to open from inside, right?"

Then we hear it. Loud barking from the cab behind the seats. Chained to the side of the cab is a gray pit bull who apparently just woke up.

"Easy, killer," Levon says, grabbing a half-full bag of onion rings from the dash. He takes one out and feeds it to the dog, whose eyes go soft as he eats.

"Stay here," Levon says to me, opening the door in the back of the cab that leads to the storage part of the truck. I look at the dog, still chomping the onion ring and licking its lips.

"Candy, come here!" Levon yells.

The dog growls, then barks again, and it startles me. I grab the onion rings and give him three. After he's done, he growls some more and lunges toward me, but there's just enough space from the end of his leash for me to sneak back to the door behind the cab. The truck is filled with cases of beer. Levon already has the back door open and a six-pack under his arm. We jump out and make a run for it.

Soon we are in another field, this one of golden wheat.

We run until we can't run any longer, panting. We have made a path through the field and are now in the center. I can picture it from above. An ocean of yellow, two dots in the center, bent over, heaving.

We eventually catch our breath.

"They'll never find us in here," I say.

"As long as the trucker won't. What the hell was he going to do, feed us to his pit bull?"

This time I kiss him, and he kisses me right back.

Chapter
21

By the time the six-pack is finished, we've made a bed of our clothes, and our bodies don't know where one ends and the other begins. I keep looking up at the stars, wondering if this is all real.

Before we fall asleep, Levon says, "Candy, there's something really important I have to tell you."

What could be more important than what he just told me with his body?

"If Jamal's dead, you can't carry that burden. Like I told you, it wasn't your fault. It was my fault. I was the one who got you into this mess."

"Well, it's a beautiful mess," I say, drifting.

I dream that I'm at a kitchen table with my mother, my father, and Levon. We are eating dinner and laughing like everything is normal. My mother is drawing a picture of my father, who is wearing a suit. Then the table becomes a boat and we are sailing in rough waters, my father at the helm and my mother standing on the bow. Levon dives in and swims away; then the water evaporates and we are stuck in a desert. My father holds a bottle of water and drinks it all himself. It starts to get really windy, and we are all swept up into the sky. I am holding my mother's hand, but her grip slowly loosens.

I wake to the piercing song of the swallows.

The beer cans are scattered around us.

Levon is crushing each one and putting them into his bag. We slowly gather up our makeshift bed and follow our path back to the rest area. The trucker is long gone. Levon gets some coffee out of the machine, and I get peanuts. We sit on a bench and wait until a woman drives up in a beat-up Subaru. Her wrists are lined with bangles, and she's wearing a tie-dyed scarf around her head. She smiles at us as she goes inside. On her way out, she stops to take us in.

"Do you kids need help?" she asks.

"Is it that obvious?" I say, and she lets out a high-pitched, birdlike laugh.

"We need a jack," Levon says.

"Oh, I had one of those but I divorced him," the lady says, proud of her joke. Then her face goes serious. "I've got the other kind of jack too."

We get into her Subaru, hoping she doesn't have a pit bull and sociopathic tendencies. She takes us to our truck, which is miraculously still on the side of the highway, with no ticket or anything. While Levon changes the tire, I sneak looks at his muscled arms. The bangle lady, who calls herself Isis, talks to me about her three dogs named Ketchup, Mustard, and Pickle. "Pickle's the bad boy," she says, "naturally."

When Levon finishes, Isis hugs us both, like we're the ones who did *her* a favor.

The next few hours pass without a word. We drive. We both know that after last night, yet another part of the game has changed. There's warmth running through my body that I can't explain. We stare at the road ahead, check the mirrors behind, and keep breathing.

Pretty soon we're in a city. Heated, sultry air swells up in waves off the sidewalk. People mingle in the pockets of shadow between the streetlights. Cars blast hip-hop, screen doors slam, street vendors sell ice cream and tacos.

"Welcome to North Miami, home of the American

dream," Levon says with his half smile. A few miles later, he pulls into the trailer park where I assume he lives. There are four trailers on each side, most with abandoned flower boxes and overturned tricycles. The ninth space at the end is just a plot of tar, as if whatever was there burned to the ground.

He shows me into his trailer, which is worse than I could've imagined. It's basically one big room with a wall for the bedroom that doesn't go up to the ceiling. All of a sudden, I feel guilty that even my dorm room is ten times nicer than this.

Levon shows me the bedroom and a picture of our fathers together, taken some years ago. I remember Wade's white sunglasses that he always used to wear.

"Wow," is all I can say.

In the corner, Levon boots up his dad's antiquated PC.

"Top of the line, huh?" Levon says.

"It's high speed, which is all that really matters."

I google Duke Bryant, Levon's dad's name, and the case comes up—the prosecutor, the detective, and everything. Since there are no pens, I get out my handheld and film the screen that has all the info.

Levon goes to the bathroom, and I log on to my new account to see if Billy Ray wrote back. He has.

From: tapwaterrocks@yahoo.com
To: gonegirlthankgod@hotmail.com
Subject: Re: omg

Candy Cane—

I was wicked happy to see your email. I went by your grandma's place, but she wasn't there. I left her some dark chocolates. Attached is an MP3 but it's rough—don't judge! Please come home for Christmas.

Love,
Billy Ray

I listen to the song, and even out of Levon's dad's dinky computer speakers, it's pretty good. Billy Ray is singing softer than he did in the band, and his voice cracks a little but in a good way. He thrums a hypnotic rhythm on an acoustic guitar and sings:

If there's a house on a hill
in the shade of a tree,

167

that's where you'll find me.
That's where I'll be.

From: gonegirlthankgod@hotmail.com
To: tapwaterrocks@yahoo.com
Subject: Re: Re: omg

Billy—

Cool song. Please check on her again.
And how did you know she likes dark
chocolate?

Candy Cane

PS I hope you have a girlfriend.

I kill the screen just as Levon comes back; then he checks
his own email. We end up sitting on the couch, staring
at the leaks from the ceiling that look like tears on a wall
that's seen too much sadness. I never cried much for my
mother or for my lack of a father, but I can feel my head
get heavy, and I lean it on Levon's shoulder. He takes me
into his arms, and then everything goes quiet. It hits me

right there that it never matters where you are or even what you've done.

It's who you're with.

Chapter 22

Let's go," Levon says, waking me up from a nap.

"Where?" My mind is so hazy that for a second I forget what we're even doing here.

"King of Diamonds."

"Oh. Right, right."

As we drive through the industrial section of downtown Miami, homeless guys crouch in storefronts and alleys.

"What was the homeless guy's name, the one that died?"

"Robert," he says. "Robert Kempler. He was a professor at Miami Dade College at one point."

"What?"

"Yeah."

"So how does one become homeless after being a professor?"

Levon gestures out to the boulevard where the shadowed people still linger, smoking and dealing drugs, some just staring into space.

"Every one of those people—or every homeless person—started out with a home and a job. They didn't grow up homeless."

Yeah, and I started out a bored boarding-school student, and now I'm an outlaw.

We scope out the King of Diamonds from across the street. It's Strip Club 101: a huge, ugly, one-story cement building painted black, with a bright-red door. A large black man with a beret sits outside the entrance on a stool.

"He never got the memo about berets," I say.

"I think it looks good on him," Levon says. "Not everyone can pull it off."

This from a guy who totally can pull off a cowbot hat, not to mention a face I could look at for a long time.

"So, are you going to ask him or should I?"

"Go for it, Black Swan," he says.

"Oh my God. Do I look like Natalie Portman with this?" I ask, rubbing my shaved head.

"Better."

I get out quickly and cross the street, trying to emanate tough journalist chick as opposed to teenage fugitive.

"Hi, I was wondering if you could help me out."

"We ain't hirin'," he says, barely looking at me. I notice a scar across the bridge of his nose and a razor-thin mustache.

"Yeah, that's me, aspiring stripper," I say.

He looks at me, then *really* looks at me, and says calmly, "What can we do for you then, young lady?"

"Whisper. I'm looking for Whisper. She used to work here?"

"Sorry, don't know anyone by that name."

"How long have you worked here?"

"What are you, my parole officer?" He dabs at his forehead with a folded bar napkin and adjusts his sunglasses.

"No, I'm a girl who's trying to help a friend."

"Miss, you need to leave now. This is a twenty-one-and-and-over establishment. And I ain't got time to be messin' with no kids."

He lowers his sunglasses and looks at me hard as he says this. Something about his dark eyes reminds me of Jamal, so I make like I'm leaving but walk around the side of the building. He follows for a few steps, but then gets a call on his cell phone.

I search for a side door or another way in.

Toward the end of the block, there's a back entrance with a cloudy cashier window. There's a woman in the little booth; fifties; curly, gray hair. She's a little blurred from the clouded glass.

"Hi."

"Well, hello there. I know you're not a customer, and don't tell me you're here about a job."

"No, I'm just looking for a friend. She used to work here. Whisper?"

She puts down the money she's counting and looks at me. I give her my big eyes and curl my mouth just so. It's what I used to do when I wanted something from my mother. It usually worked, and from the woman's sigh, I think it's working now.

"Her name is Marissa. She left us years ago, but I heard she teaches yoga now down in Sobe."

"Oh. OK, great. Do you know what the studio is called?"

The woman looks at me, incredulous.

"What is it you want from her, anyway?"

"Just answers to a couple of questions is all."

"You're not a cop?"

"I'm sixteen."

"Well, I don't know the name of the studio but it's on Eighteenth, a few blocks off the beach."

"Great. Thank you so much."

She nods but doesn't smile.

I walk back to the front and wait to cross the street. The black guy approaches me, pointing one of his thick fingers.

"Hey!"

"I'm leaving," I say, "but just FYI, you may want to rethink the beret."

I run across the street and don't look back. I get into the truck, giggling. "Step on it."

Levon starts the truck. The black guy is heading toward us.

"Hurry! Before Mr. Beret makes mincemeat out of me."

Levon pulls out in time.

"What is Sobe?" I ask him.

"South Beach."

"That's where we need to go. Eighteenth Street."

"I'm on it. What is it, her house?"

"Yoga studio."

We see two cops on the way, both parked. The first time Levon makes a noise, and the second time I do. We can't be caught now. We've come too far.

Sure enough, there's a little studio two blocks off the beach called Yogaworks. There's a class in session. The teacher is a man with a short ponytail and a thin but muscled body. As the people file out, Levon and I sit on the curb. When everyone's gone, I tell Levon to wait for me. I go inside, and the teacher is hanging up the mats. The place smells like the boys' locker room at school, but with a hint of something trying to mask it—patchouli oil?

The man sees me and smiles, tilting his head.

"Hello," he says in a singsong tone.

"Hi."

"What can I do for you?"

"Well, I'm looking for someone who teaches here. A woman named Marissa?

He smiles again, as if me coming here is perfectly natural, like everything that happens in his life is simply contributing to his bliss. I know the type; there are a lot of them in Oakland.

"And who are you?"

I try to think of a reply fast. Something other than I'm Wade Rex's kidnapped daughter.

"I have something of hers that I know she'd want. She was a friend of my father's."

He seems OK with that answer. He finishes hanging up the last mat, then grabs a towel to dab at his face.

"I'm not at liberty," he says, but I can tell he knows her. His expression gives it away. "I'm afraid you're on your own."

On my way out, I go into the girls' locker room, where a woman is toweling off next to the shower in the corner.

"Hello," she says, her face an open book.

This is my last chance. I decide to get to the point.

"Hi. I have a question. Have you been coming here a while?"

"Since it opened, why?"

"Have you ever taken a class with someone named Marissa?"

"Yes, but she no longer teaches here. I think she's at Flow in Fort Lauderdale now."

At that moment, I feel another shift, like the first crack in a wall that is flooding from within, the water starting to trickle out.

Flow.

I run to the woman and hug her, not even caring that she's wet and half-naked.

I still don't know the end of the story, but I could live off these beginnings.

Chapter
23

I t's all part of a plan, and maybe the plan was happening before we even knew it.

I'm going to take my first yoga class with Whisper, a.k.a. Marissa, to feel her out. Levon's going to see his grand-mother, whose nursing home is also near Fort Lauderdale. He drops me off, and we plan to meet up in two hours. He doesn't even think twice about leaving me. At this point, we're in this together. The issue of Jamal still lingers in the pit of my stomach—Did he die? If not, will he come after us?—but I can't change the outcome. It's too late. And the cops had no idea where we were headed, although anyone with half a brain could figure it out. But Levon is still wearing his hat, and my head is still shaved. And even though we saw a picture of the Toyota again on the news in Levon's trailer, the pickup truck has never been associated with us.

Flow Yoga has a makeshift lobby painted powder blue with cube-shaped cushion chairs. The woman behind the counter looks like she should be in one of those ads for a prescription drug that makes you happy. That is, before they mention the list of possible side effects, ending with dementia and death. She smiles at me like I'm a camera and tells me the first class is free. I put my new fake email on the sheet and check the "intermediate" box. The room is small but has a vaulted ceiling. The walls are tan, as are most of the people in the class, which is made up of young mom types, a bearded hipster, and a gay couple.

Before starting, she turns right to me and says, "So we have a new person in our group today. Welcome. Your name?"

I pause. I can't say my real name in case someone saw my story on the news.

"Rena," I say.

"Namaste," the whole class says in unison. It sounds very similar to "Have a nice day," which makes me giggle.

I pray she's not going to, like, ask me what my hobbies

are or to reveal one of my deepest fears. This is supposed to be exercise but it's feeling more like group therapy.

"OK, Rena, any health concerns I should know about?"

I shake my head, then look down at the wooden floor, willing everyone to stop staring at me. I am wearing shorts and a T-shirt, while everyone else has clothes that are basically painted on their skin. Except the hipster in baggy sweats, who smiles at me. Apparently his yoga fashion needs work as well.

During the warm-up, I steal a few peeks at Marissa. She seems so grounded, so pure, but not in a prescription-drug-ad kind of way. I'm looking for signs, cracks in her armor, but I'm having no luck. She exudes genuineness. *Is it really the same girl?*

Thankfully, I'm in the last row, so I just copy the woman in front of me, who doesn't seem that good anyway. At the end, we lie on our backs, palms open to the ceiling. Marissa rubs a stick around a metal bowl, creating a reverberating hum. She tells us, in a deeper, more intense voice, not to think about yesterday or tomorrow, just the clear emptiness of the present while our bodies restore. She talks about a ray of sunlight that came into her room that morning and how it felt like the finger of an angel. I am totally with her, but the finger part throws me, and I can hear one of the gay guys suppress laughter.

"Stay in that clear space," Marissa murmurs. "Where all the tension releases and you are a cloud, settling into the earth beneath you. Stay in that light space for as long as you want after class. Namaste."

"Namaste," everyone group-mumbles.

"Have a nice day," I whisper.

I plan to take her advice and meditate, but someone farts, and a bunch of people are rolling up their mats and rushing out. Like the fingering angel, it's kind of a buzzkill. I sit up and watch the rest of the class, some determined to stay on their backs and be a cloud, others completely back into their earthly bodies, hopping over people, taking out their phones. Marissa slinks into what looks like a closet with an orange sari for a door.

The gay couple smiles at me, as do a few of the moms, and eventually it's just myself and the bearded hipster, who chose to stay on his back meditating through all the after-class chaos. I stand up, walk over, and peek behind the sari.

It's not a closet. It's a hallway. The strong smell of incense and eucalyptus oil makes me a little dizzy. There's a faint sound of a didgeridoo coming out of hidden speakers. At the end of the hallway, there are two doors. One has a homemade sign that says "Massage in progress," with drawn hands holding the words, and the other one is cracked open.

I push it another inch. Marissa is scrolling on her cell phone while lying on a small white couch. What did she ever see in Wade? What do all those groupies really see in him? Yeah, he can sing, but he's skinny and scary looking. I'm so glad I got my mother's looks, not that I'm even half as beautiful as she was.

I knock gently, and Marissa looks up.

"Hi, sorry. I wanted to say how much I loved your class."

"Thank you," she says, sitting up, her smile betraying nothing of her past. "Come on in."

I move through the doorway and stand there awkwardly.

"I was curious… Do you just think of what to say? You know, at the end of class…"

"Yeah, it's not scripted, if that's what you mean."

"Amazing. I love the imagery." She smiles again, like I'm the breath of air she needed. I ride the wave. "And your voice, it reminds…" My face gets warm. "It reminds me of my mother, actually."

"Oh, how nice."

"You seem to have this glow, like, you clear the shadows."

"Clear the shadows. I like that."

I don't tell her that it's a line from Billy Ray's song.

181

She walks over to open the window, and as she reaches for it, the back of her shirt rises. There's a tattoo on the small of her back, a little off center. It's a poorly done butterfly.

"Well, thanks so much for the class."

"You're welcome," she says facing me again.

I start to leave but take a really deep breath and will myself to turn around.

"Marissa?"

"Yes?"

"This is awkward, but I have this project for school. I have to write about someone I admire, and I have to interview them. It's just a few questions… Maybe I could call you sometime?"

"Of course!"

Marissa writes her cell number on the back of her business card, then edges me toward the door, but I'm not ready to go yet. Not without confirming she's Whisper.

"So, this is going to sound strange, but do you like the Black Angels?"

Her eyes go dull for an instant, her cheeks reddening in a flash of shame.

"Uh, yeah. I used to. Why?"

"Just wondering. They're playing Friday, and I may have an extra ticket."

"That's really sweet of you, but I'm... Yeah, I'm busy Friday."

Marissa smiles her enlightened yoga smile. Even with the tramp stamp, she's clearly reinvented herself.

"Anyway, nice to meet you."

We smile at each other, and as I walk away, I try to picture her as a stripper, or even an escort, coming on to Levon's father in the backseat. It seems plausible, especially from her reaction when I brought up the Black Angels and the tattoo. If the friend approach doesn't work, we'll have to get some dirt on her—some reason why her present life can't know about her past one.

Levon is pulling up as I leave. I get into the truck and hand him the business card. As we drive back to the trailer park, he's silent. I can tell something's up.

"How was your grandmother?" I ask.

"She didn't recognize me."

There's water in his eyes, and I am quiet, trying to give him space. Still, part of me wants to touch him—on his cheek or behind his ear—to give him a small gesture of sympathy. I don't know how he feels, but I can imagine it. My own father barely recognized me to begin with.

I read the signs going by: beauty shop, car wash, dry

cleaners. When I glance at Levon, he blinks out two tears. I take his hand, and this time *he* grips mine tight.

"I just keep thinking how stupid my father was to believe Wade," he says. "To take his bait. That was two years he could've spent with his mother. The reason why she doesn't recognize me is because she hasn't seen him. It's too confusing."

"Did she know the circumstances? When he first went away?"

"I told her it was a mistake, that he would do his time and be a better man for it."

We drive along the canals with docks where fishing boats and whalers float, tied up until their next use.

A cop pulls out of a side street and starts following us, and I can feel heat rising in my face. Levon pulls his hand away and puts both on the wheel, gripping tightly. I can see a vein pulsing in his neck.

Not now. We are so close.

After a couple of blocks, the cop turns, and we let out a collective breath.

I try to say something, but Levon puts up his hand. His mood has darkened. How can you feel so close to someone and then the next minute so far away?

A few miles later, I tell him about Marissa, that I think she's Whisper.

"Oh yeah? Tell me this. Why would she want to dredge up that part of her life? She seems to have moved on."

"I'm working on her. She likes me. If I can gain her trust—"

"Dammit, Candy! This isn't a TV show. This is my fucking life!"

He is fuming, and I can hear my stomach rumble as I sink a little farther into the seat. We stop at a light, and outside my window, a scraggly man shakes a stained coffee cup.

"That man didn't deserve to die," I say very quietly.

Levon responds even more quietly. "I know. What about Jamal?"

We stare at each other, neither of us knowing the answer.

Chapter 24

Levon shows me his corner of the trailer, behind the makeshift wall.

"Not much, but it was home for a long time."

"You're moving out though, right?"

"That's the plan."

There are some movie posters and another picture of the girl. She looks pretty, but in a masculine way, like she might be good at softball or horseback riding. Levon catches me looking at the picture.

"She might come by later."

"That won't be awkward at all," I say, and he laughs.

He grabs us two beers from the half-size fridge. We clink, then drink. When he's halfway done with his, he speaks.

"You sure you want your own father in jail? I'm fine with getting the money. Or not, even."

"What do you mean *or not?*"

"I'm saying I...*we* don't really know what we're doing."

I love that he says *we* and means it, even though he's not being very positive.

"I do. I know what we're doing. Tomorrow we're going to the beach. And then we're going to meet up with Whisper, and one of us is going to convince her."

"What if we just get the money, on the DL. Then I put you on a plane back to your school..."

I can feel my stomach turn. He's not supposed to say this. It's not following the script. I won't end up on the cutting-room floor.

"Levon, we're in this together. You need me as much as I..."

"Calm down."

My right leg is shaking slightly, and I can feel a drop of sweat run into my ear.

"I am calm."

"Fine, we will go with your plan tomorrow, but that's it. Everything after that's an open discussion.

My grandmother has visiting hours again in the morning so...”

“I’ll go with you. I can wait in the truck if you want.”

“That’s too risky. You can come in.”

I hear some kids laughing outside. Going on with their lives. No extortion, kidnapping, murder, just kicking around a ball.

I take a long sip of my beer.

Levon goes into the bathroom, and I can hear the people in the next trailer. First they are fighting in another language—German maybe? Lots of harsh consonants. Then they are having sex. I turn up the volume on the old-school TV. It’s an ad for a credit score website. The song is actually pretty good—better than German sex sounds. By the time Levon comes out of the bathroom, the couple next door is finished, thank God.

After a while, we both get sleepy. We lie next to each other on the one double bed, not touching. Eventually, he turns and takes me into his arms. He smells like soap and beer and something else I can’t quite describe.

I sleep incredibly well, but I wake up alone. Levon is restless, doing push-ups on the trailer floor. He has turned the picture of the girl facedown, which allows me a secret smile.

I turn on the TV again, scanning all the news channels, and find a short segment about us. They are claiming both kidnappers are still "at large."

So Jamal isn't dead? Or maybe he snuck out of the hospital? The thought literally sends a chill through my blood.

Levon says he's going to get coffee and will be back in ten minutes.

After he leaves, I call NRS and ask for Mrs. B, my drama teacher. She answers in a peppy voice.

"Mrs. B here, what's the word?"

"Hi, it's Candy Rex."

"Candy! We are worried sick. Where are you? Are you OK?"

"I'm fine. It was just a prank, some friends of mine. I'll be back after break."

"What? But a witness said you were forced. Candy, is someone there with you right now?"

I see Levon through the trailer window, his T-shirt a little damp from his push-ups, getting into the beat-up truck.

"No. I'm alone. I'm fine. I have to go."

"Wait. Candy—"

"Bye."

I hang up before the call is traceable, although it's unlikely that the cops have bugged her phone.

I take a long shower, and as I'm drying off in the steamy, dated bathroom, I hear Levon come back. Through the crack in the slightly opened bathroom door, I watch him do more push-ups, his triceps forming taut ridges with each dip. Then he stretches each quad while a few drops of sweat run down his now-bare chest and over his midsection. His body should be used as a specimen of human perfection. A few minutes later, while I'm still drying off, I can hear him walk up to the other side of the door.

"You OK in there?"

I look in the mirror.

"Yes," I say in lustful tone I immediately regret.

"Great," he says.

Great what? Great, why don't you get your ass in here while I've got nothing but a towel on?

"I'll be out in a second," I say, attempting to be serious.

When I get out, he's stretching his hamstrings. I sit on the bed, suddenly unsure and exposed. The truth is, he's right. I don't really know what I'm doing—but who does the first time you try something? This could be my moment.

Our moment.

Levon stands, wipes his temple with his arm, and heads into the bathroom.

"Whoa," he says, walking into the thick steam. I bite my

tongue and wait until he shuts the door and turns on the shower to get dressed: bathing suit, jean shorts, and the T-shirt of some trucking company Levon gave me. It has his scent—woodsy but also sweet.

When he comes out, we both move in a sort of domestic dance. It's our routine. We can usually get ready to leave in seven minutes. If someone was observing on a hidden camera, it might look choreographed, but we've become a natural working unit. After today, who knows?

The nursing home looks like the one from that movie with Philip Seymour Hoffman and Laura Linney, the title of which always escapes me. A brown brick building on a nondescript street, with a measly attempt at a front yard that's overgrown and a sign with clouds in the background. You know it's bad when the sign is the prettiest thing about the place.

"Is that supposed to be heaven?" I ask.

"Anything would be better than this dump," Levon says. He parks. "Now, I'm just warning you. She's not all there."

"I get it."

We have to sign in, and Levon tells the front desk lady that I'm his cousin. As we walk down the hallway, I suddenly wish I had my handheld. A woman stands in a doorway, looking off into space, tightly gripping a teddy bear by

191

the neck, while four black guys play cards like it's any other day. Columns of light from the windows wedge in, illuminating the dust in the air. We get to Levon's grandmother's room, which has a single bed and a frosted window that is long but only a few inches wide. It doesn't open but casts a strange, sickly glow.

I am shocked by how good she looks, considering. She sits on the bed with a Bible on her lap, her black-and-gray hair cut rigidly at her shoulders. She doesn't look at either of us. There seems to be something on the opposite wall she's obsessively staring at.

"Did your father name you after the song?" I ask Levon, who nods, and at that very moment his grandmother gives me sharp look for a split second, her face coming into focus. Or maybe I imagined it.

"So you were born on Christmas Day?"

"Day after," his grandmother says, still staring straight ahead. Levon looks at her like a boy who has just found his long-lost toy.

"Gram! It's me."

"I know," she says, "but where's your brother?"

As easily as Levon perked up, he visibly deflates—the boy now realizing the toy doesn't work. It's so hard to watch that I have to look down.

"I don't have a brother, Gram."

She laughs, like he made a casual joke.

I whisper to Levon that I'll meet him outside, and this time I know she looks at me. Another razor-sharp glance, her glassy eyes alight, not unlike her grandson's.

When Levon gets in the truck, he lets out a long sigh.

"Did it go any better?" I ask.

He doesn't answer, just shakes his head slowly.

When we reach the causeway—the long bridge over the bay that connects downtown Miami to South Beach, past the cruise ships and the private island homes—I put my hand out the window again.

"She knows me at least," Levon says. "When you mentioned the song, she lit up. I think if I'm around her a lot, she'll start to come back."

"Yes! She doesn't really seem that far out of reach."

"Of course, you never know about these things."

"That's for sure," I say without adding, *like us*.

Chapter 25

South Beach is nothing like the beaches in San Francisco. For one, there are thousands of people here. It's a total scene. Women with fake boobs bursting out of their bikinis, college kids drinking warm beer, Cuban families eating meals spread on bedsheets. We go past the hotels, each with their signature umbrellas, beds, and chaise longues perfectly lined up in corresponding pastel colors. There are people selling everything: massages, necklaces, incense, bottled water, fresh fruit, brownies. Planes fly by advertising the clubs on banners flapping behind: DJ TIESTO @ LIV 11pm. TEA DANCE @ SCORE GO GO BOYS 10-CLOSE.

The sand is bright white, and the water is turquoise and pristine. It could be described as paradise, if not for the giant cruise ships invading the bay, the long industrious oil tankers billowing cylindrical clouds of smoke, and the noisy Jet Skis carving through the water, leaving snake trails of iridescent gasoline.

"Sensory overload," I say as we find a small section of sand near the surf beyond the hotels.

We sit down on the blanket from Levon's trailer and start to eat the sandwiches we picked up at the café with Planet Earth painted on its door. Mine is turkey and cheese. Levon's is roast beef. He picks the tomatoes off his and flings them onto the surrounding sand. Within seconds, some seagulls are fighting over them.

"I don't think tomatoes are good for their stomachs," I say.

"They're survivors," he says.

"Like us?" I ask, not sure what I even mean. He nods slowly. I feel that now-familiar drop in my stomach, knowing that after today, after this week, this is all going to be over. One more year of boarding school doesn't sound that appealing to me.

As if the world is responding to my thoughts, I hear the now-familiar whoop of a truncated police siren as a squad car pulls right up on the sand. My whole body goes rigid, and my breath catches. I am ready to run but locked frozen. Two cops get out of the car, walking right toward us.

Have they been following us the whole time?

Levon didn't hear the siren. His back is to the cops, and he takes another bite of his sandwich like nothing's wrong. But then he stops chewing as he notices my hands shaking and sees the look on my face.

"What the…"

The cops are two feet away. They are beefy and mean looking, with shiny handcuffs and leather holsters. They walk by so close that one of them kicks sand onto my leg. I hold my breath until they pass. The cops are headed for a drunken woman in her underwear, sipping out of a brown paper bag. They approach her, ask her questions, then one of them grips the woman under her arm and leads her away.

"Oh my God. I thought that was it. I thought they were coming for us."

The beach becomes paranoia land. We finish our sandwiches while intermittently looking over our shoulders for more cops or anyone who recognizes us. It feels like a dare to be out in the world. Still, I made that call to Mrs. B for a calculated reason. She will tell the authorities, and word will spread quickly. The story will die. I just hope she believed me.

We lie in the sun for a while. Levon goes in the water first. From behind my sunglasses, I watch the way the water glistens on the muscles of his back, the way he shakes his head when he comes to the surface. He carries himself with sensual and effortless ease. It's a shame he doesn't like cameras. They would eat up every inch of him.

As he lies back down next to me, catching his breath, our arms touch. It's intensified, like I can't feel the rest of my body.

"Levon?"

"Yeah?"

"I called the school. I said it was a prank, voluntary."

"I appreciate that, but I'm not sure—"

"Neither of us is going to jail."

The sun is so bright that I can't tell if he's smiling or squinting. He moves his arm so we are no longer touching.

"So, what about your girl? Is she down with the Albuquerque plan?"

"She doesn't know about it."

He looks at me with his impossibly bright eyes and his cute half smile.

"Well, I do," I say.

"That's true."

A big-bellied Cuban man walks by with a bulldog on a chain. The sun slides behind a cloud, and all the brilliant colors of South Beach become rendered in shadow. Then a few seconds later, the sun peeks back out from under the cloud, and it's like the electricity of the world is restored. I can't help but feel hopeful.

"What about this Billy Ray guy? He sounds cool. I like that song you played."

"He's OK," I say. "He's a good friend to me. But there are no real fireworks."

He laughs. "What do you know about fireworks?"

I think about us driving on the freeway, the window down, a rock song on the radio, him turning toward me with the tree's shadows crossing his face, the wind blowing his hair, the flickers of light in his eyes, the twisted feeling in my belly.

"A little," I say.

Chapter 26

The French café has only four tables, and two big, droopy dogs are collapsed outside. From across the street, I can see that Marissa is already there.

"OK, are you coming?"

"I don't think so," Levon says.

"OK, well, wish me luck."

When I approach the table, I notice she's halfway through a scone and what looks like iced green tea. I order a hot chocolate, which seems wrong, but what is right anymore? I'm in Miami with my kidnapper, trying to get an ex-stripper to testify so my double-crossing father can go to jail. Considering all that, ordering a hot chocolate when it's eighty degrees out seems totally normal.

"So, what's this project?" Marissa asks.

"What?"

"You said you had a school project."

I consider her, strands of her highlighted hair framing her delicate face. There is a small scar on her wrist, whitened over time. The cut is horizontal, a cry for help. A beacon of her stripper past. Yoga Woman is not fooling me, not now that I've seen the scar *and* the tramp stamp.

"Marissa, I'm not here for a school project."

She doesn't seem that surprised, like she may have known something was up.

"So, what is it then?"

"Does the date April 14, 2012, mean anything to you?"

She sips her iced tea, letting an ice cube rest in her cheek before biting down on it.

"No, not really."

"What about the name Whisper?"

Boom. That does it. An emotional lightning bolt crosses her face, and then she eyes me like I am dangerous. She checks around the café for someone who could be watching us. It's just the barista and an older gentleman in a suit with a coffee and the *Miami Times.*

She is suddenly annoyed. "What is going on? What do you want?"

"Well, remember I mentioned the Black Angels concert?"

"Yes."

"Wade Rex is my father."

"Oh...kay..."

"And I use that term loosely. He was barely a sperm donor. Anyway, on April 12, two years ago, there was an accident involving a limousine."

She gives me a blank face, not giving anything away. I try to channel the plucky journalist characters I like in so many movies.

"Listen, Marissa. Someone was killed that night, and I'm not here to implicate you in any way, but you were the only other person there."

"What are you talking about?"

"The homeless guy. He died. And my father was driving."

She's still trying to give me her game face, but it's not working. The lightning has returned. Her lip quivers; her left eye twitches. Watching her transform gives me adrenaline.

"Do you remember Duke?"

"Who?"

"The driver. He was in the back with you. We need you to testify that my father was the one driving. Would you do that for us?"

She flutters her eyes like something is caught in them, and then she stops, fixing her gaze on me.

"Who is *us*?"

"Me and Levon, Duke's son. It's a long story."

Marissa puts a ten-dollar bill on the table.

"Look, that was another lifetime for me. I'm not—"

"I know, but maybe this is a way of putting it behind you for good. Or at least to help us?"

"Why would I want to help you? I don't even know you!"

"You help people every day with yoga. You don't know all of them."

She shakes her head, gathering her things.

"Look, we are going to see the detective tomorrow. Come with us. That's all I ask."

She shakes her head like I'm being ridiculous. Then the door to the café opens, and Levon walks over to the table. They look at each other, he and Marissa, and it's like the world stops around them.

"I'm sorry… I have to go." Marissa turns to me. "I don't even remember…"

"But you do, I think. I saw it in your face," I tell her.

"Please," Levon says. "My father's been in jail for almost two years."

"And you're saying that was the night? With the limo?"

"Yes," Levon and I say in unison.

She contemplates it for a second, and then says, "So what's in it for you guys?"

"Me? Good question. Well, for one, my lame-ass father will finally have to take responsibility for being such a major douche bag, and two, my friend Levon and his dad will get what they were promised."

"Which is?"

"Another long story. Please, you have to help us."

She seems to consider the possibility again but deeper. Then she snaps back. "I'm sorry. I can't."

As she gets up to leave, I grab her forearm, and I can feel the fist of my heart clenching, my eyesight clouding over with tears. "It's the right thing to do, Marissa."

"What do you know about right and wrong?"

"We've done a lot of wrong to get here," Levon says. "But I think we all know this is right."

She stares at him.

Is she seeing his father in him? Whatever it is, it's working.

Marissa sits back down, sighing loudly.

"I guess I could do it," she says. "But I'll need money. To pay off the loan for my yoga studio. Five grand."

"Wait a second. You're blackmailing us?" I say.

"Fine," Levon says, like he was expecting to pay her off.

I figure she doesn't know about the million, so five grand is no big deal.

"As long as I'm not exposed, you know, in the media."

"No, it will all be under wraps," I say. I've never said *under wraps* in my life.

Marissa turns to Levon. "You know, there were a lot of things I did back then," she says. "Weeks went by that I couldn't remember. But I remember your father." She looks at him, her eyes unwavering. "He was different. He had so much light. That shouldn't have happened to him. I'm sorry."

"It's not your fault," Levon says.

The way they are talking to each other, it's like I'm not even there, and feeling the need to make myself known, I touch Marissa's arm again, this time softly.

"I'll text you, and we'll come get you tomorrow?"

"OK," she says, not taking her eyes off Levon.

I excuse myself to let whatever needs to play out between them happen and make my way to the tiny but quaint bathroom in the back. There are flowers in a water glass on the sink, like someone just picked them outside and put them there. I look in the mirror, trying to see my mother, trying to see myself as an adult. I splash my face and look again, attempting to see what Levon sees.

When I get back to the table, Marissa's gone.

"She said she'll see us tomorrow," Levon says.

"Great."

We don't say anything for a bit. I finish my hot chocolate, and he drinks Marissa's water in one long gulp.

"I'm so glad you came. I was losing big time until you walked in."

"I had a feeling," he says, smiling.

I smile back but then have to look away. The feeling is too intense, like getting too close to a fire. I breathe deeply without being obvious about it.

Then I hear my name.

It's TMZ, being watched by the bored barista chick.

They are calling it a hoax and saying I'm no longer in danger.

"Well, at least we can show up backstage and not cause a scene."

Levon nods, but I know he's still thinking what I'm thinking.

Jamal.

When Harvey Levin adds that the suspect is still under scrutiny and both of us are wanted for resisting arrest, Levon winces, gets up, and leaves, and I follow.

Isn't the boy supposed to follow the girl?

"There are no rules," I say when we get into the truck. "There is only justice. Our plan is working."

On the way back to the trailer park, the clouds are low and menacing, threatening to press against the earth. We pass a car wash where teenagers are smearing soap suds on each other. It doesn't seem like they know life is complicated; they're living in the moment.

Inside the trailer, we watch the news and there's nothing on our story. Now that it's been labeled a hoax, it's completely gone. The media are savages, devouring you until your story is just a corpse on the side of the road, left to decay. But wouldn't they want to know if a certain rock star covered up his role in a major crime? Harvey Levin would take that call.

"You know, she still may chicken out," Levon says.

"Well, what's plan B then?"

"You tell me."

"We show up and bluff him. Tell him we've talked to Whisper and the authorities. We get your money, and we—you—ride off into the sunset and open your movie theater."

Levon's face glazes over a little, as if the dream is possible, but then he turns concerned, like a boy who might lose a friend. "What about you?"

I don't think about what I'm going to say. I just look at

his handsome, humble, and kind face, and the words come out. "Well, I could come with you."

He gives nothing away, just ponders the thought.

He grabs a stash of whiskey from under the sink and pours us each two fingers. We start watching *America's Funniest Home Videos.* We are on our own sides of the bed, but we laugh at the same videos. For the next half hour, there is no absent father, no sick grandmother, no kidnapping, no accidental murder. Just two people, a little lost, sharing a space in the world.

Chapter 27

When I wake up, Levon is gone.

Something about the ruffle of the covers on his side makes me think he has made a getaway. *Did he freak out that I wanted to go with him?* There's an indentation on the bed where his body was. I sit up and press my hand on the mattress: still warm. I peek in the bathroom: empty. I look around the trailer, and the infamous green backpack is nowhere to be found. I'm not sure which is sadder, the empty pint of whiskey with the Dixie cup facedown over the top of it or the warm, unmade bed with no one in it.

I wash my face and put on one of the two outfits I've been

wearing the whole time. My hair's starting to grow back a little, but I don't care. I start to film the trailer, and I'm not sure why. Maybe because sad things can be beautiful.

I put on my gas station sunglasses, take a deep breath, and walk outside. My heart swells when I see the truck. Levon is sitting in the driver's seat, patiently waiting for me. I run toward the truck like it's my newborn child. I get in and look over at him, but his expression is grim.

"What's up?"

"Leeza just came over. You missed her."

"That's her name? Leeza?"

"Yeah, why?"

"Nothing."

"Anyway, she said there's a video of us in some restaurant that's gone viral."

"What? I'm not even on social media. Are you?"

"She put me on Facebook and Twitter. I don't even check them."

"That's kind of weird."

"I know."

"You never really told me. Is she your girlfriend or—"

"Candy, the point is she's going to take the video down, untag it or whatever the hell. In the meantime, we've got to work fast."

"OK."

We drive to Marissa's little, pink house that sits on one of the canals. There's a big palm tree in front of it, and unbeknownst to her, I film her leaving, gathering her hair in one hand, throwing it over her shoulder. She's wearing jeans and a T-shirt and still looks stunning. I will file the shot under ex-stripper yoga teacher who blackmailed us.

She gets in, and I slide into the middle. She hands Levon a plastic bag, and he pulls out a black jacket. Levon holds it up in front of him like it's some kind of miracle, which it kind of is.

"My dad's jacket."

"I didn't think I still had it, but I checked the back of my closet and there it was. He gave it to me 'cause it was chilly that night."

"Thank you," Levon says, his eyes shining.

"All right, let's do this," I say.

They both look at each other, sharing another moment I'm not going to pretend to know anything about. When we pull up behind a Dumpster near the precinct, I quickly brief her before she gets out.

"OK, his name is Colin Price. What you need to do is go with the rock-star angle. If you told him Joe Schmo was driving the car, he wouldn't care, but if you lead with Wade

Rex, he'll be all over it. Tell him it's been bugging you for a while, that you feel like the truth needs to come out."

Marissa looks skeptical, like she might bail on the whole endeavor.

"Listen, just because my father's a rock star doesn't mean he can get away with murder. Justice needs to be served, Marissa." That sounded like a line from a TV show, so I go for a more personal approach. "For Duke, Marissa."

She raises her hands and sighs. "How can I be sure I won't get dragged in—as an accessory or something?"

"I already researched it," I tell her. "It was vehicular manslaughter, so as long as you weren't driving, you'll be fine."

"OK."

She gets out and heads toward the precinct, and I notice Levon checking out her backside. Really? I could never hold up to someone like Marissa. She is beautiful. Me, I'm cute if anything. A sinking feeling overcomes me.

"Candy, what's wrong?" Levon asks.

It's gotten to the point where neither of us can have a dark thought without the other one noticing.

"Nothing. I don't want this to end."

"What?"

"I mean, I want you to get your money and help your family, and I want my father to go to jail, but then what?

211

I go back to school? This trip has made me feel more alive than ever. This is going to sound stupid, but I think I have an adventurous spirit."

Levon laughs. "That doesn't sound stupid. And it doesn't mean you won't have other adventures. Just, hopefully, legal ones..."

"I really, really wish my mother were alive. Everything was an adventure for her. She'd help me figure this out."

He puts his hand on mine.

"Sorry, Candy. You know that I brought you into this mess."

I look at his eyes, those bright pools of green.

"Are you kidding me? It's the best thing that's ever happened to me."

He smiles, and I can sense a weight lifting off him, like he's finally believing me, like my plan might work. As he kisses me, I pray to whatever God is up there that it does.

When Marissa gets back, she seems a little shaken. She gets in and tells Levon to start driving. After a minute, she starts talking.

"You're right. His whole demeanor changed at your father's name. He asked me if I knew where you two were. I said I saw you, and you seemed fine, but I didn't know where you were staying."

"Great. OK, what else?"

"He made a call and found out the angle of the surveillance cameras. There are two—one outside the bank and another in a streetlight. He ordered the footage. He said it was cut and dry, that the tapes will tell him everything. If it shows your father driving, he will reopen the case. He said he would call me as soon as he knew anything."

"I knew it."

I can feel blood rush to my head and my fingertips, my whole body filling with endorphins. It's happening. All three of us are smiling as we turn onto Collins Avenue.

"I'm curious though," Marissa says to me as we pull up to her house. "How bad could your father have been that you want him in jail?"

"He's never really been a father. Honestly, it might even be good for him."

"Well, for what it's worth, Wade was always nice to me."

As she gets out and walks away, I think about the truck crash, the whipped cream in the desert, the giant peace sign. The one time I ever shared a real moment with him. His eyes were wild, and he picked me up when we finished, held me as he spun in circles. It was like this dormant person had finally woken up. But what about all the time we missed? How many more fun things could we have done together?

Why did he abandon me? What the hell was so wrong with me? I've spent my whole life asking that question, and maybe, just maybe, putting him away will make all those questions disappear for good.

As we drive back to the trailer, I watch people on Rollerblades, tourists with wide-brimmed hats, vagabonds with elaborate signs. The world goes on. *But what does that mean for me and Levon? And where is Jamal? Is he out of the hospital? Does he have a posse that will come after us?*

All I know is that, for the first time since my mother died, I feel needed and like I'm affecting change. All those movies I've watched have come in handy. I'm not sure where that will leave me. Hopefully not in jail with my father.

Levon glances over at me, and I almost can't take it. The magnet is stronger than ever. I look out the window but immediately am pulled back toward him. I lean my head against his shoulder, and he lifts his arm up and over me. I fit perfectly.

I breathe in his scent and close my eyes, trusting him to steer.

This was not an accident.

I am in the right place.

Chapter
28

I call Rena from the front porch of Levon's trailer, which is more like a large step. She picks up on the first ring.

"Hi, Rena. It's me. How are you feeling?"

She says something in Russian and lets out her weary sigh. Although it's slightly annoying, I'm happy to know she's behaving like herself.

"They say it is hoax now."

"Yes. I'll be back to school when break is over, so don't worry about me."

"Your little friend, he comes here now, every day. We play cards."

"Billy Ray?"

"Yes. He is good boy."

I think about Billy Ray and Rena playing cards, and I can't help but smile. Still, it's like looking at an old photograph, faded at the edges. For all of her shortcomings, Rena did raise me. And Billy Ray gave my heart a test drive. But now they both seem parts of a different life, a picture I barely recognize. I feel like this whole adventure has propelled me into a different chapter. I don't know how it will end, but who ever does?

"There's something else I need to tell you, Rena."

"What is it, child?"

How do I tell her that her son is basically a murderer and going to jail?

"Not that we ever see him, but your son, Wade, is going away for a while. He's done something terribly wrong."

Again, she mumbles something in Russian.

"What?"

"He's not my son."

I shake my head to make sure I heard her correctly.

"What?"

"You heard me, I think."

What the hell is she talking about? I know my mom's parents died when she was young, and my grandfather on Wade's side was killed in the war, but...

216

"So what does that make you exactly then, Rena?"

"I'm still grandmother, just not with blood."

"Were you planning on keeping this from me forever? It's kind of information that's relevant. This is crazy. Where's my real grandmother?"

"She was my sister."

That actually makes sense. Rena's sister was a documentary filmmaker in Russia. I've seen her films. They were not translated, so I couldn't understand anything, but they were shot beautifully.

"Is she still alive?"

"No. That's why I took you in."

"Well, nothing like a real heart-to-heart chat."

"What?"

"Nothing. I always wondered why you didn't really care that Wade never came to see you. And why you had no baby pictures of him. It makes sense. But why tell me now?"

"Because you are old enough. You're becoming adult."

"Yeah, whatever that is."

"Strong girl. You don't need me anymore."

Maybe she's right.

"Now, Candy, Wade is not saint, but you be careful. Stay away trouble."

"I'll try to, Rena."

"And call Billy. He is good boy. Misses you."

"I'm glad he's keeping you company."

"I'm OK. I'm old but OK."

"Good."

This is where she usually hangs up without saying good-bye, but instead I hear her say my name softly.

"Candy."

"Yes?"

"Blood, it does not matter."

"I know, I know."

But I don't know. I really don't.

&

On our way to the Fillmore, where the Black Angels are playing tonight, I fill Levon in on what I'm calling a *little tidbit* of info.

"So, I officially have no family, besides Wade. Great prospects, huh?"

"Yes, but your grandmother is—"

"Still my grandmother, but not. Technically my great-aunt. You know the weird part?"

"What?"

"I'm kind of happy about it. I know I can be dark, but that woman is like a black hole."

"But she said she loved you."

"She does, in her way, I guess. But get this... My real grandmother? She's dead, but she was a documentary filmmaker. Maybe that's where that gene comes from."

"Makes sense."

We pull up to the art deco facade of the venue, the words *Black Angels—Sold Out* in lights. The *A* on *Angel* is crooked. I tell Levon it's metaphoric, but I don't think he knows the word. We pull into the alley around back, where the trash cans are ripe and the asphalt is pocked with potholes and covered with oil stains and random bits of trash. Out front—the Easter egg–blue columns and the bored teenager in the miniscule ticket booth—that's what the Fillmore looks like to the world. Back here is the real story. The roadies are loading in, and all of it, even the smell of the Dumpsters, makes me yearn for my childhood. The crew is dressed mostly in black. They have beards and bandanas, sweat patches in the armpits of their T-shirts, and probably girlfriends at home they can't commit to. The band is nowhere to be seen.

Levon checks out the roadies moving lights and speakers, cords and mic stands. I want him to have what he wants.

Whatever that is. My father's money. A movie theater in Albuquerque. Me.

"Mom," Levon says.

"What?"

"The road manager—his name is Mom. Or they call him Mom. I remember him. He watched me a few times."

"Is he there?"

"Yeah, hang on. Wait here."

Our pickup is blocking the alley, but no one else is back here except the huge, dirty, white truck with the band's equipment, its hazards blinking yellow. I get into the driver's seat of our truck, touching the steering wheel, the armrest, all the things Levon had touched.

I watch him talk to the Mom guy. They do a bro handshake and laugh a little. A few minutes later they high-five, and Levon starts to walk toward the truck. I quickly scoot back into the passenger seat before he notices.

He gets in. "Wade told him my dad went to Thailand."

"Figures."

He pulls out of the alley and onto the street. A crowd is starting to form—misfit kids and bald guys with tattoos, cougars dressed younger than they should be, sorority girls with way too much lip gloss.

"Mom says the band will be there in an hour and to come back then."

As we drive up Collins to kill time, the anticipation swirls thick in the air around us. This is it. It's happening. But what exactly? It's like everything has led up to this point, but how the hell are we going to actually do it?

Levon pulls back down the alley behind the venue and turns off the ignition.

"OK, what's your brilliant plan now?" he asks.

"Well, I think we should confront him. What do we have to lose? C'mon," I say with a little bit of force. "We are here."

Mom is potbellied, with a mustache and a tiny, greasy ponytail. He looks like an overgrown rat. I give him my best smile and tell him who I am. He says he knows and opens the door to let us in, staying outside to smoke his cigarette.

Inside, there are several dressing rooms, but one huge one has a printed sheet of paper stuck to the door that says *Wade Rex.*

Levon gives me a quick nod.

Then I open the door.

Chapter
29

The room is all white—the walls, the columns, the curtains that section off a private area, the couches. There is a giant piece of art framed in black wood, a completely white canvas except for a smudge of red. It looks eerie, like a stumbling, bleeding person accidentally brushed against it.

My father is in the corner, and there are two girls, one on either side of him—a redhead and a brunette. (According to *Us Weekly*, he doesn't like blonds.) It's so clichéd, like the set of a boring music video. He is smoking a joint and blowing the smoke in a thin stream into the redhead's mouth. They are so in their own world that they don't even notice us standing there. Levon looks catatonic. "It's cool," I whisper to him. "I got this."

"Hey, Dad!" I say, pretending I'm really excited to see him. "It's me, Candy! Your daughter!"

Wade stands up, his jaw slack. He is still very skinny and hasn't aged well since I last saw him on TV. I go to give him a high five but pull my hand away at the last second. He smirks like a moron.

"I see you're still living the rock-star life. Where'd you get these two?" I say, pointing at the girls. "Bimbos R Us?"

The girls curl back like frightened animals, then grab their stuff and leave. It's not like I'm holding a gun or anything. Although that would be way more Tarantino.

"Candy, what are you doing here? And what happened to your hair?"

"I thought we could have a little family time."

"Can you stop with the act, please?" He takes a step back and actually gives me a once-over. "You're looking fine, by the way."

That's when Levon steps forward and punches my father in the face.

The punch propels Wade back onto the couch and it tips over, leaving his black cowboy boots dangling in the air. I turn to Levon. He looks charged, like a superhero that has gained unnatural power. "I've been waiting two years for that," he says under his breath.

A huge bodyguard with a bald head and shiny silver spikes through his eyebrows appears out of nowhere and grabs Levon forcefully, bending his arm behind his back. As tough as I know Levon is, this guy could break his arm like it was a pencil.

"Hey!" I yell.

Levon looks up at the guy, still reeling from the punch, his eyes wide, temples pulsing.

Wade gets up slowly, holding his face. There's a thin streak of blood running down his hand.

"You brought him here?" Wade asks me.

"Other way around."

"What happened? I was worried about you," he says.

I let out a sharp laugh. "Who needs to cut the act now?"

"I'm serious."

The bodyguard says, "Wade, you need to get that cleaned up. I'll take care of this punk."

"Wait!" I say, following the bodyguard, who drags Levon down the hall into another smaller room. The door shuts, and I hear a loud shuffling sound, Levon gasping.

I bang on the door.

"Don't hurt him!"

I run back into my father's dressing room.

"What is he doing to him?" I yell at Wade.

"Duke's kid was the one who kidnapped you?"

"That's not relevant anymore. I wanted to be with him. I love him, actually. How about that? Oh, I forgot, you don't know anything about love. Your vacuous rock songs have names like 'Spill It on Me.'"

His eyes are red, and he's breathing heavy like a dog.

"I loved your mother," he says.

"That's great, Wade, but what about me?"

He tries to hug me, and I push him away.

"What is he doing to Levon? Tell him to let him go!"

He holds up his arms like it's out of his hands now, which of course it isn't. He probably knows exactly what *take care of this punk* means.

"It's a free country. You can't contain him."

"He just fucking *assaulted* me, Candy."

"You deserved it. You looked at me like I was another one of your…"

As if on cue, the brunette returns and starts cleaning up Wade's cut.

"Listen, Wade, I know everything. I know about the limousine, about Whisper, about the money you promised

Duke, and how you blew him off after he went to jail for you for two years."

Wade is acting like I'm telling him he forgot to tip a waitress. The brunette is acting like she's not listening, but she's hanging on every word.

"Is that what he told you?" Wade asks, like it's some ridiculous story.

"Yes, and I believe him. And you *will* pay."

Wade swats the brunette away, rights the couch, and sits on it. Then she starts dabbing at the wound again.

"Candy, he *kidnapped* you."

"It was consensual."

"There's no such thing," Wade says.

"So you're not going to pay?"

"Not now, not after he kidnaps my fucking daughter."

"Why would you even care? I haven't seen you in years."

"Candy, let's not start this now."

"It's cool, Wade. I don't need to see you. This, all of this, is pretty depressing. You're an aging rock star who dates girls my age." The brunette—who's probably in her midtwenties—smiles, obviously flattered by the comparison.

"You're going to have to pay for living your life like a spoiled child, for using the people around you like pawns."

As quickly as it came, the brunette's smile disappears.

"How do you think you can go to that fancy school of yours? I *work*, Candy."

"If you want to call it that. But all the money in the world doesn't make up for you not being able to take your head out of your ass and actually care about someone. My mother died, and you just dropped me off."

I told myself I wasn't going to cry, but I can't help it. A switch gets turned on inside me, generating tears like they're on tap.

The brunette places the Band-Aid above Wade's eye, and it looks pathetic. It's not fixing anything. A metaphor if I've ever seen one.

"You look like her," Wade says.

"Well, I'm glad I don't look like you, *Night of the Living Dead*."

The brunette drops her jaw. Apparently that was going too far. I give her a look that says *You have no idea how far I can go.*

"Candy, I'm not paying someone a million dollars for kidnapping my daughter. You could've been killed."

"Like you would even care. You left me with Rena, which was kind of like dying anyway. By the way, I know she's not my grandmother. Not that it would've mattered.

You would have left me anywhere. Face it, Wade. You just don't give a shit. You never have."

The brunette leaves, shaking her head on the way out, and another woman—in her forties but dressed kind of slutty—comes in. She starts to put makeup on Wade's face.

"Tell them to let Levon go. Now!"

Wade starts to lift his arms again and I look at him, my eyes burning.

A stagehand with a headset comes in and says, "Wade, I need you in the wings."

Screw it. I will get Levon myself, with or without Wade's help.

"Candy," he says as I walk toward the door. "You need money to go back to Connecticut?"

"It's Massachusetts, fucktard."

I go down the hall to the other door. It's locked, and there's a guy standing guard. He's got spiked, black hair and blurry tattoos on his arms.

"You can't do this," I tell the guy.

"I'm just watching the door, young lady. I don't see or hear anything."

"Levon?" I say to the door.

I hear him mumble something inaudibly.

"I'm going to get you out of there, Levon. Hang on."

The guy smiles at me like, *yeah right.*

Our disposable phone, which I have on me, buzzes.

It's a text from Marissa.

> I tried to call you but there's no voice mail
> detective price said case is reopened

I let out a yelp.

"Oh my God."

Another text comes in, which I read with a surge of happiness to Levon through the door.

> footage shows wade driving car
> I won't have to testify

Mr. Bad Tattoo, who's drinking from a pint bottle, lifts an eyebrow.

"Wade is onstage," I say through the door. "I'm going to get your money if it's the last thing I do. Then I'm going to get you out of here. By the way, nice right hook."

I take off, giving Mr. Bad Tattoo my best scowl.

Backstage is a maze of hallways and rooms. I find what seems like another main backstage room. It's huge, and there's a vintage bathtub filled with ice, champagne bottle arms sticking out of it. Various people are sitting around on their phones. Through the walls, I can hear the Black Angels' first song, my father scream-singing, the pounding bass, and the roaring whine of electric guitar. No one even bothers to say hi to me. I walk down the one hallway I haven't been down yet.

There are two other tiny rooms. In one, a couple sleazily makes out. In another, a black briefcase sits next to a laptop. The briefcase is locked. It's a four-number combination. I make a few random attempts, and then it comes to me: 1989. It's a song on the Black Angels' first record. The case clicks open, but nothing is in there except a passport (belonging to the goon bodyguard, from before he stuck metal through his eyebrows), some gum, and a Swiss Army knife.

Before I shut it, I notice a manila folder with what looks like a bunch of contracts inside it. As I pull it out, I gasp at what I see underneath it: a checkbook with the words *Black Angels LLC* on the top. I know the company; it's where my trust fund comes from, the very checks Rena gets to pay for me. I rip one off, replace the checkbook just where it was, and shut the briefcase, randomizing the numbers. I fill out the check for one million dollars with a pen that has a half-naked girl on it. I fold the check in half, put it in my back pocket, and walk back down the hall.

The kissing couple is now on the floor, and they have broken a lamp. Back in the huge room, someone has fainted, and three people are hovering over her. I go up to the side of the stage to watch, hiding behind a curtain so the goon, who is on the other side of the stage in the wings, doesn't see me.

My father is in his hectic, frazzled, stage persona mode, shaking his hair and dragging the mic stand. It occurs to me that it is the one thing he does well. It is entertaining to watch him, even though I know the real story behind him, the one that VH1 or E! would never run. Liam, the bass player, looks kind of bored, and the drummer is sweating profusely. The guitar player, a new replacement for the old one who died of liver cancer, looks out of place—younger and definitely green. He is happy in a way that suggests he can't believe his fate. His goofy look says *I'm playing with the Black Angels!*

After the song ends, the applause is deafening.

It's time for the drum solo, so everyone else exits stage right except for Wade, who walks over to stage left where I'm standing. I know this—he always exits stage left.

I hold out the check and the half-naked-girl pen and say, "Sign it. It's the right thing to do. The guy has spent two years in *jail*."

He looks at me. He's exhausted. Makeup is streaming down his face. His matted hair is in disarray.

"I read somewhere you're worth seventy million. You can afford one for Levon and his father."

"Candy, where did you get this?"

"Doesn't matter. What matters is that you deliver on your word. That's what makes someone a man."

He looks at me. The crowd roars louder. The stagehand runs up and says, "Wade, you're coming back, right?"

"Yes, hang on."

He sighs, and his eyes turn sad. He looks so tired that I half expect him to collapse. But instead, he says, "Sorry," and turns back into the bright lights, the crowd screaming harder than ever.

Chapter

30

O n stage right, the goon's eyebrow spikes glint in the low light from the stage. I make my way behind the curtains and creep up behind him, stand on my tiptoes, and whisper in his ear.

"Let him go, or I'm calling the cops."

He smiles like that's an absurdity, which it kind of is. I don't want Levon anywhere near the cops.

"You can't hold him against his will."

"Just giving him a message," the goon says. "You don't punch Wade Rex in the face."

"Yes, you do, actually. He did."

The band breaks into "Spill It on Me," and again, deafening screams.

I make my way back toward the room where they're keeping Levon. There are more and more people backstage. Lots of older girls. One of them says, "Hey! Are you OK?" recognizing me even with my shaved head. I ignore her and keep moving.

Mr. Bad Tattoo is not only passed out; he's also snoring, still holding the empty bottle of cheap gin. *What kind of low-rent bodyguard is this guy? But I'm not complaining.*

I grab the key on the wooden stick next to Mr. Bad Tattoo and use it to open the door as quietly as possible. Levon looks fine, other than the duct tape on his mouth and wrists. This time I bite the tape off *his* wrists. Then I rip the tape off his mouth and he huffs loudly. Mr. Bad Tattoo wakes up for a second and then falls back asleep. We tiptoe out of there and run into Mom in the main hallway.

"Dude, I have to ask you to leave," he says to Levon. "Heard what happened."

I turn to Levon and say, "I got this. I'll meet you at the truck."

Mom guides Levon out the back. Better than being bound and gagged.

All I need is a signature. I'm so close.

The band finishes, and they all pile off the stage. The raging sea of applause and screams is louder than it's been all night, if that's even possible. The band passes right by me. As they walk by, the smell gets more and more pungent, until the sweaty, disheveled drummer brings up the rear. I turn and follow them into the main dressing room.

The bass player, Liam, who's been in the band since day one, recognizes me. He's gotten kind of fat, but he actually looks younger and healthier than the rest of them. The new guitar player still has that goofy smile. Various people—press, groupie girls, and roadies—mill around the room. Mom is trying to relegate them to one side while the band members wipe their faces and catch their breath. Liam comes right over to me.

"You are so big! I remember when you were this tall," he says, pointing to his knee. "You were the coolest kid, so chill. What happened to your hair?"

"It's a fugitive thing. I remember you, Liam. We used to make Kool-Aid."

"Yes, and we didn't spike it, thankfully."

"Not until I went to bed."

He laughs but then looks at me inquisitively, as if drawing some sort of conclusion. "It's crazy how fast time moves."

"Sometimes. But then again, at boarding school, an hour can seem like a day."

He laughs again, and there is a glint in his worn but kind eyes. A ding goes off in my head. I beckon him to follow me, and we end up in the opening act's dressing room, now abandoned and strewn with empty beer cans. We sit on a faded-red love seat that has some sort of sticky substance on it.

"Glamorous, huh?"

"Well, you of all people know," Liam says, "it's never really glamorous."

"Yeah. In fact, sometimes it can get ugly, like the limo crash."

He tries to act like he doesn't know what I'm talking about, but that doesn't work. The cheer drains from his eyes, and he slowly shakes his head. "Is that why you're here?"

"Look, you knew Duke, right? Wade's driver?"

"Met him a couple of times. Before he crashed the limo."

"That's just it, Liam. It was Wade who crashed the limo. He told Duke to take the rap and he'd pay him a million dollars. Well, Duke did his time, and of course Wade blew him off. I can't let that happen, and I need you to help me."

I take out the check, written in Levon's name, for one million.

Liam looks shocked.

"C'mon, we all know Wade is capable of this."

A wave of sickness curls through my stomach, knowing I'm related to him. *Was Rena right about blood not mattering?*

"I need you to get Wade to sign this. He listens to you."

Liam runs a hand through the receding hair that falls to his shoulders. Inside all of the hard wear and tear is a nervous little boy who knows I'm right.

"What's going on here?" Wade is standing in the hallway, a towel around his neck like a rock-and-roll prizefighter.

I take out the check again and hold up the half-naked-girl pen.

Liam motions for Wade to sign it, but before he can, three cops come up from behind. For a second, I think they're coming for me, for what happened with Jamal, but then I remember Marissa's text. It was only a matter of time—and in this case, no time at all. One of the cops says, "Wade Rex?"

I point to my father.

"You have the right to remain silent…"

They cuff him and take him away, all while he stares at me. For a second, and only a second, I think about stopping them, but it's too late.

I clutch the unsigned check in my hand.

"I hope you enjoyed that show," I say under my breath.

"'Cause it may have been your last."

Chapter
31

I push open the back door and start running through the alley as fast as I can. By the time I get to the truck, I'm panting, about to pass out. But Levon's not there.

Then I hear a voice behind me.

"Easy, killer."

It's Levon, holding a cup of coffee and smiling.

"You're OK?"

"Yeah." He's still got residue from the duct tape on his cheek. I use the sleeve of my hoodie to get it off.

After we get in the truck, I turn and show him the unsigned check.

"I was so close, Levon. But they arrested him. Turns out Colin Price works fast."

"Fuck." His face falls.

"But we'll figure it out."

We look at each other, realizing that getting a million dollars was probably not likely in the first place.

"Mom gave me five hundred in cash. Let's stay in a nice hotel tonight."

"OK," he says.

We choose the Raleigh, an old-school art deco place where the pool is shaped like a giant lily and looks like something out of a Busby Berkeley film. The valet with the vintage cap gives our pickup truck a once-over.

The suites are all booked, but we get a room on the seventh floor on the ocean side. The interior is art deco classy, done in pale pinks and cream. There are fresh flowers and a deep soaking tub. Behind the floor-to-ceiling glass is a white balcony, and beyond that, a study in blue, shade after shade blending into one another. It's a far cry from the dumps we've been staying in. We order room service and watch *The Godfather* On Demand. I think back to when I first quoted the film and Levon couldn't believe it. It seems like a lifetime ago. I try not to think about what happens next. *Going back to school? Going to sleep without the sound of Levon's soft snore?*

The food is amazing—crispy calamari and fancy salads, grilled fish and risotto, and some cheese I can't pronounce.

When the movie ends, Levon gets up to go to the bathroom, and as we pass each other, he hugs me—a little more tightly than expected—and I wish time would stop. I want to stay there forever, his strong arms around me, the credits rolling.

"You'll get your money," I tell him.

"It's cool, even if I don't. At least he's going to pay for what he did."

"And what about Jamal?"

"Well, they're gonna find me eventually. If he died in the hospital, I'll tell them I saw it, that it was self-defense."

"You would do that for me?"

"Yes."

"What else would you do for me?"

He kisses me hard, and we fall onto the bed. He explores my body, running his lips down my sternum, kissing my hips. It is way better than our wheat-field moment. In the field we were urgent, almost desperate. Now we are slow and sweet, almost dreamlike.

We fall asleep spooning. I dream that we are driving in a convertible by the sea, and the wind is in our hair. He is smiling, laughing, and we're having a blast. The sun shines into the car. But when I move in to kiss him, the car sails off the edge, *Thelma and Louise* style.

When I wake up, I'm sweating. Levon is already up, presumably getting coffee. I rinse off in the shower and walk out onto the terrace and look at the Atlantic. A kiteboarder is jumping the waves, catching serious air. The hotel workers are putting out the beds and the chaise longues and planting the umbrellas. Levon comes to the door in shorts and a T-shirt, coffee in hand. It is a different feeling, looking at him this way. He's the definition of sexy guy, while Billy Ray is just a cute boy. *Where does that leave me? Girl, woman, somewhere in between? What about this Leeza girl? I have to believe she doesn't mean that much to him, based on what happened last night.*

Levon lets me borrow the old laptop he got from the trailer to download the footage from my handheld. He's got an old version of iMovie, but I know how to navigate it. While he goes for a swim, I start to assemble a little movie. I decide to give it a Vine feel, a bunch of tiny clips strung together. The first shot is of the trees in Massachusetts, naked branches outside the car window. Then my first confession, which he actually didn't erase, followed by the Tappan Zee Bridge, its spires jutting out of the cold, shiny river. Various motel people and the shots of Levon he didn't know I took: his torso washed in the light of the TV, his hair blowing in and out of his eyes, his muscled arms contracting as he gripped the wheel, his firm backside walking into the Comfort Inn lobby.

There are some close-ups of stains on motel bathroom walls, paper cups of whiskey, and a weathered bible. There is only one other shot of me, from below. I must have had the camera on without knowing it. I'm looking out the window and Levon is talking. It's night, and the streetlights flash the car periodically, like an urban heartbeat. I can't hear what he's saying, but a smile pokes at the corner of my mouth.

As the shots go on, there's more daylight and everything becomes bright white and blue—the sky, the clouds, the sea, and the sand. There are pastel buildings and the burst of green from a palm tree, but they're all in the foreground of the blue and white. There's Marissa in her feigned elegance, and the crumpled sheets and the empty pint of whiskey in Levon's trailer. The last shot is of Levon's grandmother sitting on her bed. She tilts her head a little, seemingly content.

As the film is rendering, I walk onto the balcony. There are more people out, and a group of birds circle an upended trash can. A few minutes later, Levon comes back and says, "How's it going, Scorsese?"

The small hotel towel barely covers his lean waist, and his arms still gleam with seawater.

"Tarantino, more like it. I used a song you had in your library, some band called Elbow."

"Ah. That's my dad's favorite band."

I play the movie, and it comes out pretty good for an amateur road-trip, day-in-the-life thing. The song works really well, almost like the images are explaining the lyrics:

I come back here from time to time.

I shelter here some days.

At the end, Levon turns and looks at me with his spotlight eyes and kisses me. Then he walks to the edge of the balcony.

I move up behind him so that I'm only inches away. I can see the tiny pulse in his neck and smell the sea mixed with fancy soap. I put my arms slowly and carefully around his torso, bend my face in profile against his strong back, and hold on.

Chapter
32

The story is everywhere. Blowing up on Twitter, TMZ, blogs, and newspapers. Wade Rex is being charged with vehicular manslaughter from the reopened case two years ago. The rest of the Black Angels' tour will be canceled.

My father's going to jail.

I can't believe our plan worked, but part of me feels a pang of shame. *What if he gets hurt or raped? What if blood does matter? What if Levon and his dad never get the money they deserve?*

I hold the purple section of *USA Today* up for Levon to see the giant headline: Rock Star Hit-and-Run Resurfaces.

"We did it, Levon. We did it!"

"So it's official, huh?"

"Yeah, it's on, like, every news channel. So what now?"

"Well, I talked to Billy Ray," he says.

The balloon of elation I am feeling gets immediately punctured.

"What?"

He puts on his serious face, his eyes glazing over a little.

"He called earlier, right before our phone died for good. When you were taking a shower. Your grandmother's in the hospital. She's stable, but he bought you a ticket from Miami to Oakland. You leave in a few hours."

Something in his tone sets me off.

"Oh, now you're going to play responsible adult?"

He turns his head and runs a hand through his hair. "Well, what do *you* want to happen, Candy? Why don't you tell me that."

"I don't know. It just sucks all this has to end."

"Candy, I know it was an adventure for you, and it was for me too, but it was also a way for me to get a life. And to help my dad."

"So I'm not a part of it anymore? You're just going to erase me like my father did? That's cool. I'm used to it."

I can't even stand in front of him right now. I want

to throw something or scream, but instead I walk into the hallway and down the stairs, slowly and methodically. In the lobby, I ask the concierge if I can use their phone. He sets me up at my own desk and tells me to press nine to get an outside line. I know it's weird that I know Fin's number by heart, but I do. He answers on the fifth ring.

"I did it, Fin. We did it. I put my own father in jail."

"Candy, wow. It's nice to hear your voice."

I fill him in on everything, including the fact that Levon is starting to break my heart.

"Wait a second, you fell for this guy?"

"Beyond. The other guy he was with was mean and violent, but Levon is sweet and protective. We bonded. It's hard to explain."

"Well, as long as he's good to you."

"He is—he was. I love him, Fin. And he's acting like it's all over now, that I just have to leave. I mean, Rena's in the hospital so I know I have to go but still. God, I feel so stupid right now. I just stormed out of our room."

"Candy, you're too smart to pull that. I get it's been tough for you. It's tough for a lot of people. But you have an edge over most people in the world 'cause you're smart, really smart. This might seem like the end of the world or whatever, but it's only the beginning. You can really do something with your life."

"Like be a filmmaker?"

"Of course! Now go up there and be adult about it. Let things marinate."

"Did you just say *marinate*?"

Fin laughs. "Yes, and I don't think I've ever used that word before."

"Unless you were talking about steaks."

He laughs again. "Anyway…if it's meant to be, he'll come around. Sometimes our relationships are like braids. They come apart and then back together again."

I listen to him breathing. I realize in that instant that Fin's the closest thing to a father I've ever known.

"Yeah, well, sometimes it sucks being young, you know?"

"Ha! It sucks being old too."

I know that Fin doesn't have it so great. He has no money, and there's something dark about his past, but he loves fishing and his dog. Simple things. Is that what Levon wants? A movie theater and a dog? What about me?

"Well, I'll see you when the semester starts."

"Yes, I hope so. No more kidnappings, OK?"

"OK."

I say good-bye and take the elevator back upstairs. When

I get to the room, Levon is at the window, watching the ocean. He turns and opens his arms. I walk into them. We hug, but it doesn't feel the same.

When we break apart, he says, "Listen, you helped me, Candy. And even though it was scary and a little crazy, you made it fun. But this, we…"

"Like a meteor, right? Shines a light, then it's gone?"

He sighs.

"Is it Leeza?"

"No. Well, I don't know…"

I look at him, his face stern but with that undeniable boyishness, but something is missing. *How could I have been so wrong? It wasn't just me; there was a two-way current. It was electric. Last night in the middle of the night, when he turned and pulled me close, the heat of his skin, his lips on my neck. How could he deny that? Now, he looks like he's trying to grab at some rope that's not strong enough to hold him up.*

"Candy, don't think I'm not going to miss you."

"I *know* I'm going to miss you."

The maid comes in to clean the room, not knowing we are there. When she sees us, she bows and turns, heading back out the door.

"Hey, let me take you to my favorite place," Levon says. "Before we go to the airport."

I stand up and force a smile.

"OK."

As we start to get our stuff together, I confess to having second thoughts about my father being in jail.

"Seriously?"

"Yes."

"Candy, I'm sure they'll make some deal to shorten his time. He's a celebrity."

It physically hurts to pack up my stuff for the last time. Why can't Levon skip the airport, and we just drive on to another motel that could be the seediest of all—and it wouldn't matter?

You're never close to someone until you've run from the cops together.

I consider telling him this as he drives us through midtown, then another ten miles west of the city. Eventually we pull into a massive graveyard of cars, covering at least two square miles. Some of the cars are stacked five high, their old, broken bodies collapsing into one another. We park, then get out and sneak under a bent-up part of the fence. For a minute, it feels like Fin is right—the adventure is only beginning. We walk down the one path in the center, gazing at the rust, the scraps of metal, the shredded tires, and the mangled license plates.

"Strangely beautiful," I say.

Levon gets that playful look—when the worry and edge evaporates from his face, and what is left is simple, pure happiness. "Beautifully strange."

I take his hand and lean on him a little as we walk all the way to the other end where there's a small hill.

Don't go away from me.

We sit on top of the hill and look back on the sea of ruined cars, once shiny and purring like animals, once smelling like sex and leather and gasoline. Now crippled beyond return.

"How many babies were made in these cars, you think?"

Levon lets out his bark-laugh. "A lot."

On our way back, we stop and sit on the hood of an old Cadillac that was probably red at one time but is now weathered to brown.

"Well, maybe we can meet up somewhere," I say, but the words sound weak coming out of my mouth.

"Yeah, I'll probably stick around here awhile to make sure my father's cool. And Gram too."

"She seemed really happy to see you. She didn't show it, but you knew what she was thinking."

He smiles and shakes the hair out of his eyes. A gesture I could never ever get tired of watching. It starts to rain a little so we head back to the truck. We drive to the airport in silence and park. Inside the terminal, I go up to the counter and get my boarding pass. While Levon goes to the bathroom, I look around: a mother scolds her child, an obese guy nods off, and a girl puts on makeup while her boyfriend plays a video game. Levon comes back and asks me if I have someone to pick me up on the other end.

"I can take a bus or whatever."

I try to talk like everything is normal, like I'm not collapsing inside, like my heart isn't shattering right in front of him.

"Oh, that reminds me."

He hands me a twenty-dollar bill, and I actually laugh.

"Story of my life. All money, no love."

"Stop."

I can't look at him anymore. If I look, it will be like free falling.

He reaches into his bag and pulls out Mortimer and Randolph, which he must have grabbed from the dash of the truck. He holds them both in front of me.

"We'll each keep one," he says. "Do you want the frog or the alligator?"

"Definitely the frog, 'cause I'm foolish."

He hugs me, and I know this is it. This is where I walk away.

But I don't let go.

And neither does he.

Why is everything telling me we are still meant to be? Why am I about to leave him without even a plan to see him again?

We break apart, and I look into his eyes.

"I'm so glad you kid—"

"Shh."

"When will I see you again?"

My voice is thin, shaky. I'm the girl who is about to walk away, leaving the only person that I've ever felt like myself around.

"I don't know, Candy."

I can't stop the blood rushing into my face, the hot tears slipping from my eyes.

"You felt it too, Levon. You can't fake what we shared. Right?"

I want to yell at everyone walking by like it's just another day at the airport, with no idea that the road I was riding on is now cracking, splitting right beneath my feet. Underneath is quicksand.

Levon is not answering. He's looking everywhere but into my eyes, and for a second he looks ugly, like he just ate something terrible.

The road is ending at a brick wall, the ocean is drying

up, the sky is closing in, the air is getting thinner. And thinner.

At last he turns to me and opens his arms once again. I step into them. But the pain of knowing it might be the last time is like a choke hold on my heart. I squeeze him harder while travelers filter around us, each one oblivious to our road, our story.

But there is no road. There is no chance.

The picture is blurring.

We release, and I turn, looking back once.

There is no us.

Walking through security, I hear people talking around me but not the actual words. There is an electric hum throughout my body—a very slight ringing in my ears. It doesn't stop until I'm on the plane, staring out at the tarmac. The dry, exposed pavement is burning in this heat. I turn to face the woman who sat down next to me. She has this moment of recognition, realizing I'm a kid. She gives me a look that says *How sweet. She doesn't know anything about the world yet.*

I thought I did, but I'm not so sure anymore.

18
Months Later

There's a letter sitting on my bed in my dorm room with my name written on it in the scribbled handwriting of my father. I look at it, then slip it into the bottom drawer of my desk. There were others, but I threw them all away without opening them. For some reason, I keep this one.

I turn on my laptop and open my inbox. It's mostly filled with emails from Billy Ray. We spent last summer together and it was fun, although he knows that my heart lives in the land of Levon, whose last email was from two months ago, even though I've read it a million times.

From: Levonthedownlow@gmail.com
To: candyfromastranger@gmail.com
Subject: Re: Mortimer and Randolph

Candy—

Sorry I've been out of touch. My grandmother passed away last week. She spent most of her last few months with my father, and she was actually sharp at the end. She mentioned you!

I'm getting closer to making Albuquerque a reality. It's like a light at the end of a tunnel, I guess.

I think about our trip a lot. If I had to choose anyone to kidnap again (which I won't), it would definitely be you. I heard from my buddy at the trailer park that Jamal is now in rehab. Let's hope that lasts.

I hope school is going well. I'll write more soon but I'm caught up in dealing with my grandmother's service and packing, blah-blah-blah.

Onward.

Love,
Levon

He typed *love.* I'm not sure what that even is, but my heart seizes every time I read it. One word with so much power. I responded immediately, hinting about us getting together again, which I've basically been doing since Miami, but haven't heard back yet.

Billy Ray was very skeptical about Levon. When I got back to Oakland, I noticed right away that Billy Ray was acting like he was part of my family, which he kind of is but not in the way he was thinking. He thought we were going to be *together* together. We hung out at the hospital with Rena, and she would become so animated around him that I sensed she wanted the same thing. It was nice to see, but it also made me a little jealous. Would she have bonded more with me if I were a boy?

On the day before Rena was well enough to come home, Billy Ray and I were having our favorite pizza at the place with the old jukebox. He'd put on this Dylan song that had connected us (we'd actually sang it together once, sappy I know), and I knew it was coming. He tried to kiss me, right between bites of pizza, and I turned my face away. It felt like my former self, the one that played with Billy Ray at the train tracks and in his father's shed, was no longer accessible. I wasn't playing anymore. Feeling the way I did about Levon was like finally making it to an almost impossible level on a video game. I couldn't go back.

The Borings turned out to be the Not So Borings. Like the car graveyard Levon took me to, everything is interesting if you look closer. Right now, Brittany is telling me about the guy she dated last summer.

"He rides a Vespa, like one of the vintage ones from Europe, reads poetry, and surfs. His hair is naturally highlighted—and get this: he totally listens to what you're saying. You have to go for that type of guys. The ones who have empathy. Most guys are *so* emotionally closed off."

"I saw Levon cry twice."

"Yeah, from everything you told me, he seems like a super snack."

"Fritos go with lunch," Jiwa adds, looking up from her book. As usual, she's studying, and Brittany and I are talking.

"Jiwa, did you tell Candy about your uncle?"

"He works with Tarantino," Jiwa says, like he was some guy who lived on her street.

"No way," I say, kind of sounding like them but not caring anymore. Even Fin is happy I now have friends my own age.

"You can meet him this summer. Maybe he can help," Jiwa says.

"That's amazing, but I can't fathom how that would happen without me self-combusting or fainting or both."

Brittany laughs.

"Are you gonna bail on college and try to work in the film industry?"

"That's the plan, I guess."

I can tell they're slightly mortified, since they are still obsessed with college, but things are different now. They are trying to accept me, and it feels good. I'm still an out-sider, but I'm connected to them now. I was lame for judging them and not being more open to our differences. They still iron their pajamas, but now I'm kind of fasci-nated by it.

A week later, I finally hear back from Levon.

From: Levonthedownlow@gmail.com
To: candyfromastranger@gmail.com
Subject: Re: Re: Re: Mortimer and Randolph

Candy—

I'm in Albuquerque. My lease on the theater starts Tuesday.

Leaving Miami was chaotic, and adjusting here is the same.

More soon.
Levon

He didn't say *love* this time. Just *more soon*. Was he just in a rush? Did he bring Leeza there with him? The questions fly around my head like angry bees.

~

When I visit Fin on our usual day, I help him wash his car and tell him about Levon moving and not saying *love* in the last email.

"I think you should meet up with him sometime, face-to-face. That's easier than email, even though some people are afraid of it," Fin says. "But you're a person who needs direct contact, I think. The way you process things is very immediate."

"Yeah? How do you know me so well?"

"Trust me," Fin says, wringing out his oversize sponge, "I know more than you think."

I grab the hose and spray the suds off the license plate.

"I have a daughter too," Fin says over the water sound. "My ex, she took her away. I haven't seen her since the nineties. I think about her every day."

I can't believe Fin hasn't told me about this. He did mention something about his past, but a daughter? My jaw drops, and I stop the hose.

"I thought…"

He pulls a picture out of his wallet. The girl is around four, with a big smile and blond curls.

"Fin, she's beautiful. Did you ever try to find her?"

"Still trying. I'm saving up to hire a private detective."

"Wow."

We wash some more for a while and then start to rinse. The suds clear away, revealing a shiny, clean surface underneath.

"Did Levon and his dad ever get the money?" Fin asks.

"Yes. Wade finally paid him—on his own. I like to think I had a big part in that."

"You have a big part in everything you do, Candy. And you're gonna do great things."

"What about you? Is this it for you? Cleaning the halls at NRS and fishing?"

Fin grabs the hose from me. "Hey, don't judge."

"You should find your daughter—or at least a nice lady to be with."

Fin laughs and sprays me a little. Then his eyes get glassy, and he looks off into the distance.

"You had one, didn't you?"

"Yes, but she got away."

"I know how that goes," I say. "But guess what?" The thought comes to me as I say it. "I'm gonna go. I'm just gonna go. To Albuquerque. After graduation, on my way back to California."

Fin nods, like he's expecting me to do just that.

"You're right. I need to see him face-to-face. I know there's something he couldn't say to me at the airport in Miami."

"A girl's gotta do what a girl's gotta do," Fin says.

"Do you think I'm foolish?"

"No, more like strong."

When we finish and his truck is all dry, he gives me an ice cream sandwich and says, "Now, go pick on someone your own size."

I smile, grateful for Fin. He always looked out for me. But now it's time to look after myself.

⌒

What helped me not think about Levon every second of the day was making the film about Gary, the homeless war veteran who is supersmart but can't get a job or rent an apartment. I tried to really capture him with the content and also the light, movement, and sound. I used two of Billy Ray's songs and a song from Gary's favorite band, Steely Dan. Gary didn't want compensation and still thinks I work for CNN. I got him to sign a waiver, and I'll be doing a screening in the student theater tomorrow.

I've thought about my father a lot, even though I

discarded his letters. I know that he delayed going to jail for as long as possible, and that he recently got out on good behavior. I've had many moments when I wanted to take it back, to let him go free. But it was all too late.

Back in my dorm room, something tells me it's time. I open my bottom drawer and take out the letter.

Dear Candy,

I hope you've been getting my letters, but even if you aren't, it helps to just write them.

When you were little, you laughed at everything. You loved to stick your head out the window and watch the trees go by. Everyone told us we shouldn't raise a baby on the road, and maybe they were right, but you were really happy. You probably don't remember this, but the times you actually did cry, which was usually late at night or when you woke up on the bus, the only thing that would calm you down was me singing to you. When I'd finish the song, you'd say, "Nother song." I learned all these kids' songs, cool ones for adults too. I still know them.

Wait a second, he *did* sing to me? I have no recollection.

> You took your first step in Boulder, Colorado. Your first word was "Momma," then "juice." When you said "juice," we freaked out. My bandmates were like, "We get it. She knows a word." But it was more than that. We thought you were absolutely brilliant, which you are. Much smarter than I ever was or will be. You got your brains from your mother. Did you know she turned down a scholarship to Columbia University?

I look out at the quad, covered in a blanket of green leaves. A teacher and his wife are walking their floppy Labrador, and the sun's long arms reach through the pines. It feels like something frozen inside me is starting to thaw. I look back down and read the second page.

> I was angry with you for a while, but you were right. I needed to pay for what I did. I only wish that instead, I was someone you looked up to. You did at one time. We were a team, the three of us. But when your

mother died, well, life happened. Instead of getting closer to you, I made the choice to distance myself. I went on tour without you and never came back. I'm so sorry.

Love,
Wade

I walk over to my bed and lie down, staring at ceiling. I place the letter over my heart and close my eyes.

⌒

I sneak into the very last row of the student theater just as my film starts to show. Not that I would know, but it feels sort of like giving birth, starting with the opening sequence, which shows Gary doing his morning ritual—shaking out his blankets, brushing his teeth using water from a plastic gallon milk jug, then wrapping his various possessions in a large tarp and hiding it near the train tracks. Billy Ray's song works well. Hearing his voice makes me feel bad about the pizza place and the attempted kiss. I told him flat-out that I wanted to just be friends, that being with Levon changed everything for me.

"What does he have that I don't?" Billy Ray had asked.

"I don't know," I said, and I didn't. But I think now I'm starting to. Something is pulling me. I already have one foot in New Mexico.

There are about forty people in the theater, including the Not Borings, Fin, Max the Goth (who has since forgiven me and helped me on location), and a bunch of junior boys who were required to come for a class.

People laugh at moments that I never thought would be funny: Gary getting caught in the closing door of a bus, his skinny dog peeing a yellow stream on the sidewalk. In general, it feels like it's going well. Gary is charming on camera, and during his weekly "poetry slam," he and other homeless guys (and some college students) read their poetry and discuss it.

Aside from bouts of talking to himself, he spends his days collecting cans, bumming cigarettes, and going on about "Sara with no *H*," a girl who may or may not be imaginary. Apparently she saved his life twice, wore black leather, and played the cello. Gary always had the sense that she could show up at any minute. Toward the end of the film, underneath the covered bridge downtown, Gary cries, staring at the camera openly. It makes me think of my father's letter.

The last frame is Gary, holding a black balloon and

walking up Main Street in Northampton. He leans down to give the balloon to a little girl. At first the girl is reluctant, but something happens, a connection between Gary's bracing smile and the little girl's big eyes. She walks away holding the balloon, but after a few steps, she releases it into the sky, watching it go.

The screen goes white and, as promised, it reads:

**THERE'S SOMETHING ABOUT GARY
A FILM BY CANDY REX
DEDICATED TO SARA WITH NO *H***

People clap.

I let everyone leave without seeing me. Then, as I'm walking out, I notice someone on the side of the balcony. His hair's short, and he's wearing a jean jacket.

"That was amazing, Candy. You made that?"

"Wade?"

"Better than anything I've ever done."

"What are you doing here?"

"I got out last week. Basically came right here." His smile is a little maniacal.

"Well, they need the theater back. Let's go."

I can't believe he showed up. I immediately take him off

campus in case anyone recognizes him. We go to a coffee shop that's in an old Airstream trailer. There are no customers, just the pale girl who works there, who makes us coffees and then continues to paint her nails, glancing up at Wade. I go to the bathroom, and when I come back, Wade's signing a napkin for her.

"Seriously?" I say, and the girl looks embarrassed.

We sit at the one table outside the trailer. I'm not sure how I feel about him being here. I'm nervous, so I start talking.

"We have a few days off before finals. They call them reading days, but no one reads. They usually go online and mess around. Try to find beer. Some of the townies will buy for kids." My nerves are making me babble, and I don't care what I say because it just feels good to talk. "There's some guy speaking at our graduation. Like, some Navy SEAL who lost a limb or something. Sounds clichéd to me, but whatever."

Wade is smiling, and now there's water in his eyes. I can't look at him for too long, so I look down at my hands and keep talking.

"I'm not going to college, at least not right away. I want to make films, so if I do, it will be film school anyway. But I've read a lot about it, and you can learn more by actually working on films, so I might try to do that."

I can't tell him about my plan to stop in Albuquerque; it seems way too personal. Instead I ask him about jail.

"What was it like?"

"Monotonous."

"Did you play music?"

"There was a piano, but no guitar. I think I might do a solo record next. Even though I'm an old man."

Looking at him, my stomach sinks. I feel terrible for doing what I did.

"Well, if there's one thing about Black Angels fans, they're loyal. I think a scandal and a comeback may even work in your favor."

He smiles a little more naturally now. That's easier to look at. There's no entourage, no white leather pants, and no arrogance. He's completely humbled, like an old dog that has finally come home, waiting on the doorstep.

"How is Duke's kid?" he wants to know.

I try to act normal about it.

"He's good. He moved to Albuquerque."

Wade contemplates that while a woman in a polka-dot dress and platform shoes walks by, getting pulled by a fat bulldog.

"So, were you famous in jail too?"

"Not really. Some of the guards slipped me junk food

and stuff. But I'm just a guy, you know? A guy who screwed up."

I look at him. He doesn't seem like a rock star, even though he signed a napkin for that girl, who is now probably texting all her friends. He's right. He's just a guy.

As the sun dips below the trailer and a chill bites the air, I have a sobering thought. It's something I have always known but didn't want to believe. I had shoved it into the depths of my own denial. Seeing him in this state makes it bob to the surface: *He's all I've got.*

Yes, I have Rena, but I think she's done all she can. When I left for school, she told me that I was a woman now.

"What does that mean exactly?" I asked her.

"You don't need me anymore."

I started to get choked up, but I wasn't sad. I realized that she did her best, and that one person can't be everything to someone.

"You know what, Rena? I was so pissed when I got here and you asked me to rake the leaves. But I get it now. I get that whatever your story was shaped who you are, and I know you aren't perfect, but I did need you. I needed you a lot."

She looked away, and I thought I saw her eyes moisten.

"That is why I never told you," she said. "I wanted you

to need me, to feel like you had a real family member to take your care."

"I did, Rena. Like you said, it doesn't matter if we aren't blood related. You'll always be my grandmother, the one that raised me."

"What about your boy, Billy Ray?"

"Well, hopefully he'll realize I'm not trying to break his heart. I'm just moving on."

"He is very good people."

"I know, Rena, I know. But he feels like a stepping-stone, you know?"

"I have a feeling you'll have plenty of those."

I hugged her, and for the first time she really hugged me back.

Rena will always be my family. So will Fin and Billy Ray.

But Levon is still the giant question mark in the sky, the dream I'm still dreaming. Then there's Wade, this meek man in front of me, the one who made me. He messed up royally, but I can feel that he wants to make things better, that he's for real this time.

"Tell me about Mom. Why didn't she take her scholarship?"

He stares off into space for a second, then turns back with a new, gentler smile. "She didn't like institutions. She didn't want to be labeled a Columbia grad. She was writing a book, freehand, in all these journals. They were in my garage. I brought them, and I'd like you to have them."

I picture the mother I knew. Flowers in her hair, that ethereal presence, how it seemed everything in the world held promise to her. I don't remember any journals.

"Did she write them before I was born?"

"Mostly. And when you were really little."

"How did you meet?"

His eyes glaze over again, then he starts to talk languidly, as if recalling a dream.

"I was practicing a song in an alley, in Marin County. The band was inside the venue, sound checking. We weren't big then. I could go anywhere. So I was playing this new song I was working on. And when I finished, I heard someone clapping. I looked up, and there was your mother, in the window of an apartment in the next building. She stuck her head out, and we talked for a little bit. She had that smile, one I'd never seen before. You have it too."

Something gathers in his throat, and he puts his head in his hands. I let him cry softly, trying not to give in myself. The girl comes out to see if we need anything else but then quickly turns around. After he calms down, he takes a deep breath and looks at me, almost like he's about to beg for his life.

"You are all that's left of her and me. I know I've been a shitty father, but I want to know you. I want to be in your life. I can't take back what I've done, but I can change things going forward."

"We'll see," I say.

I think he must actually have a heart, because I swear I can hear it beating.

I lean closer to him.

"So what happened after that? With Mom?"

"We were about to head out on a European tour. I asked her to come, and she said yes. It was easy, really. Everything was always easy with her."

I contemplate asking him about the truck accident at Joshua Tree, if he remembers the giant whipped-cream peace sign we made, but I stop myself. I'd rather have faith that he remembers. I'm not sure I can handle it if he doesn't. It's my one memory of him, like a small gold stone in a river of gray ones. I want to preserve its color.

Graduation day is really hot. From the top row, the bleachers look like a sea of maroon gowns, with programs being used as fans, flipping like the wings of white birds. The Navy

SEAL, who also has a gay son, gives a touching speech. In the end, he says, "The only thing you should be intolerant of is intolerance."

Wade is like all the other parents, beaming and clapping when I get my diploma. Mrs. B takes a selfie with him, and I don't cringe. When it's time for him to leave, he tells me to come live with him in Miami, if I want.

"Really?"

"Really."

"I'm not sure about that, but I'll think about it. Thanks."

I watch him get smaller and smaller from my window as he walks away.

"Dad," I say softly under my breath. Although it's not second nature, the word doesn't feel like another language either.

I am leaving for Albuquerque in my favorite dark-blue dress. My hair has completely grown back. I have my HD handheld video camera, my laptop, my mom's journals, a few changes of clothes, and Randolph the frog.

When I hug Brittany, she says, "Go get him, but don't be desperate."

Jiwa, who always smells like flowers, says, "Be you. That's who everyone loves. And keep in touch."

Mr. Keller, my film teacher, asks me to send him a digital copy of *There's Something About Gary* because he wants to enter it in the New England Student Film Festival.

Fin takes me to the airport, and it's not as hard as I thought it would be saying good-bye. It's like he'll always be there. I know we will cross paths again.

"Promise me this," Fin says. "When you have your big premiere in Hollywood, you invite me."

"Yeah right."

"No *yeah rights* anymore! How about yeah, *that's* right."

"OK, yeah, that's right. There'll be a chair with your name on it. And one next to it for your daughter."

Before I walk into the terminal, we stand facing each other on the sidewalk. People with their own stories, their own risks, walking around us, oblivious to ours. But we are a strong fixture in that chaos. Two people who needed to come together, who shared four years of hanging out. Now it is time for all that to change. I hand him a Post-it with my email address, since he's finally started doing email. He shakes his head, like he can't believe I made it this far. I know what he means. We do one last fist-bump explosion, and I hoist my bag over my shoulder and head through the automatic doors.

I sleep for most of the plane ride, waking as we make our descent. My eyes focus on the flight attendant's cart in the aisle next to me, and I see two mini bottles of Dewar's, the whiskey Levon likes. I steal one and slide it into my bag.

The Albuquerque airport is tiny, and there are make-shift stores selling turquoise jewelry and magnets. On the way into town, I can see that Levon was right. The sky is huge. There are walls of red buttes with dense clouds curling over their tops like tablecloths. The taxi driver is American Indian and has a very intricate dashboard with taped pictures and inspirational sayings.

"You here for the festival?"

"No," I say, not knowing what he's talking about.

The road gets smaller, and more trees appear along the side. Ahead, 585 Solar Road is a small adobe house with a circular drive.

I get out of the cab and just stand there, staring at the house. There's a small garden out front that has been neglected, which might be a good sign. *If a girl were here, wouldn't she plant flowers?*

There's no car in the driveway.

I walk slowly toward the house.

I feel older. Much older than that day I was shoved into a red Toyota.

I cup my hands to the window and look inside. His jacket is laid over the kitchen chair. Our trip floods back into me, the fear and the adventure, the highways and the motels, the candlelit silo, the field of tall wheat where we first made love.

There's a lone coffee mug on the table.

I knock, but no one answers.

And he shall be Levon,

and he shall be a good man.

I sit down on the driveway and lean against the sun-soaked garage door.

Then my breath catches when I see them.

Hundreds, *hundreds*, of hot-air balloons in every color, bulbous and bright, floating gracefully in irregular patterns under an impossibly vast blue sky. The beauty of the scene travels behind my eyes and down my arms and into the tips of my fingers. I think about getting out my camera but decide against it. Some things are meant to be experienced in real life.

After a few minutes, the hot-air balloons are gone, and there is only sky.

I keep looking, waiting for another miracle.

Acknowledgments

I first must thank my wonderful friend and agent Christopher Schelling of Selectric Artists, who put a lot of effort into making the book you're holding a reality.

Also, my editor Annette Pollert-Morgan, who immediately fell in love with the character of Candy and who, along with her clever team at Sourcebooks, helped me in shaping the final product. It takes a village.

I wrote most of this book on my bed, next to my French bulldog, who would sometimes place his head on the keyboard for attention. Oliver, I would give you the moon if I could reach it.

Lastly, to Steve: thanks for being my other half, for supporting all of my creative endeavors, and for your kindness. I couldn't do it without you.

About the Author

Stewart Lewis is a singer-songwriter who lives in Washington, DC, and Nantucket Massachusetts. Stewart's previous young adult novels, *You Have Seven Messages* and *The Secret Ingredient*, were published by Delacorte Press. For more information, please visit stewartlewis.com.